Stella's Heart Code

Crawdad Beach Series (Book 5)

Lisa Buffaloe

Stella's Heart Code

John 15:11 Publications

No artificial intelligence was used in the writing of this book. This novel is a work of fiction. Names, characters, places, towns, bakeries, bakery owners, Cybersecurity specialists, software security specialists, private security companies, business owners, ethical hackers, spies, assassins, government agencies, military personnel, crawdads, and all people and incidents are the product of the author's active imagination and used fictitiously. Any resemblance to actual events, persons living or dead, or any other person, including any place or thing, is entirely coincidental and beyond the author's intent.

No crawdads were injured in the making of this novel.

Visit the author's website at https://lisabuffaloe.com.

ISBN: 978-1-957715-26-1 (eBook)
ISBN: 978-1-957715-27-8 (Paperback)
ISBN: 978-1-957715-28-5 (Hardcover)

Image by Micha, Photo by Donna Naquin on Pixabay Cover design, Lisa Buffaloe

WELCOME
to
Crawdad Beach
South Carolina

Stella's Heart Code

Tormented for decades by a man who wanted her dead, Stella Nicely moved to Crawdad Beach and prayed that God would rescue her and give her a new life. An orphan, widow, and retired cybersecurity spy, she didn't have many options other than trying to survive. She trusted God to protect her life, but could she trust Him to protect her heart?

Security specialist Wilder Templeton regretted much of his past. God had mercifully forgiven him and given him a new start. However, would Wilder be able to protect and convince the woman he had always loved that he was a changed man?

Book 5 of the Crawdad Beach Series.

Table of Contents

Chapter 1

Assessing the latest cyber threat, Stella Nicely scrutinized the computer screens in front of her. A flicker on one of her monitors jerked her attention to the security camera feed in front of her home. The screen went black.

Not sure if she should groan or growl, Stella sent an encrypted message to her friend. She'd already alerted Marcus Patterson to be careful when he returned from his honeymoon. Stella hated contacting him, but the young man might not have been born because of a mission she had been on thirty years ago.

Marcus's dad, Robert, had taken a bullet, but Stella lost part of her freedom. Someday, maybe she could go back to using her real name. She'd used so many aliases over her lifetime that it was hard to remember the name they put on her original birth certificate. Not that it mattered anymore since, as far as she knew, all her family was gone. Stella sighed. Being an orphan, widow, and retired cybersecurity spy didn't leave her many options other than trying to survive.

Baretta M9 in hand, she left her office, walked through her small den, and peered out the front window. Although it was only ten-thirty at night, no cars were passing on her street, no barking dogs, even the crickets seemed to be sleeping. Crawdad Beach slumbered in peace.

An unusual shifting of a shadow drew Stella's attention. Before she could react, two rapid flashes lit the area. Stella chuckled; her friend had arrived.

Headlights off, a black-paneled van pulled into Stella's driveway. A few minutes later, the vehicle drove away. The alarm beeped, signaling it had been turned off. Hurrying to the back door, Stella waited.

Dressed in black from head to toe, her friend stepped inside and turned the alarm back on. Removing her gloves, she narrowed her gray eyes. "You didn't need to contact me. You could have handled the situation yourself."

"I knew you were on your way. Besides that, I know you enjoy that sort of thing much more than I do." Stella grinned at her amazingly fit friend who, at sixty-five, could lift more weights than men half her age and still looked like she was in her late forties.

"It's not a big deal." Her friend pulled off her black stocking cap and ran a hand through her spiky silver hair. "You keep taking care of cyber problems, and I'll handle the human problems. Plus, it's easy to eliminate a threat with a taser."

"Were there two people, or did you zap someone twice?"

Crossing to the refrigerator, her friend took out a water bottle and gave her a sly smile. "What's the use of having just one taser when I can use two? Besides that, there were two creeps. The way they were watching the place proved they were not professionals." She sighed. "It's so hard to get good help these days. Wilder took care of them for us."

Thus, the black van. Stella smiled at the mention of their friend. Wilder Templeton's good looks favored Sean Connery. As a result, Wilder had left many women with broken hearts. "How's he doing?"

"Still never married, just getting older like the rest of us, but strong as an ox. Since Wilder runs his private security company, he'll have a nice little chat with our visitors." Her friend took a long drink of water and gave Stella a mischievous grin. "Maybe we can talk him into moving here and joining us."

Ignoring the comment, Stella followed her friend as she walked through the family room and down the hall, where she keyed in the code to her section of the house.

Stella entered behind her. "It would be good to see Wilder again." The thought made her want to cry and laugh at the same time. She'd missed seeing Wilder. He'd been her late husband's best friend but had kept his distance for the last year, almost like he was avoiding her. "Did you tell him your latest name?

"Not yet. I just decided a few minutes ago. I will be Mia Burns."

"Interesting. So, why that name?" Stella couldn't wait to hear about this one.

Mia's skin tone revealed the beautiful blend of her various ethnicities, making her the preferred agent in many missions around the world. She placed her tasers on her dresser, followed by her gun and the knife she always carried.

"One of the meanings behind Mia is the guardian of justice, and as for the Burns surname, I like thinking of putting the burn on those who try to get in our way." She chuckled. "It's much better than your choice of Stella Nicely. How dull and boring."

Stella shrugged. "The name seemed to fit with Crawdad Beach."

"You're already getting attached to the little town. You need to remember why we're here." Mia had insisted on coming with Stella as her roommate for a few months or until the threat was eliminated, but she made it clear she would be moving on after that time.

"Maybe after we take care of things, I can stay."

"Right." Mia scoffed. "Like that's going to happen. Besides, would you want to be bored in a small town like this?"

"A little more relaxed would be nice." Stella looked away. She did want to settle down and start a new life. She felt led to make the change by selling her house in Maryland, not just as a temporary stop in Crawdad Beach.

Mia took clothes out of her dresser. "Did Marcus and Olivia return home safely?"

Stella nodded. "Yes, they got in about an hour ago."

"Did they decide on his or her place?" Mia stepped into her bathroom to change.

Stella stood outside the closed door. "Marcus felt that they would stay in her building in the apartment above the bakery since Olivia would be getting up early to prepare her pastries each morning before she opens."

"I think that's wise. Olivia has an extra bedroom where he can work at his cybersecurity job. How's our boy doing?"

"He's great and head over heels with his new wife. They're happy and perfect for one another."

The bathroom door opened, and Mia, dressed in sweatpants and a t-shirt, stretched her arms above her. "You still haven't told Marcus we've been keeping an eye on him since he was born, have you?"

Stella shook her head. "No, I don't want him to be paranoid."

"You better pray we can eliminate the threat on both of your lives before too long. We aren't getting any younger. Hopefully, Wilder will have luck discussing the situation with our unwelcome visitors."

"I hope so. Plus, if all goes well, the software I'm designing with Marcus should be ready in a few days."

Mia raised a perfectly arched eyebrow. "Marcus still thinks you're designing the program to stop hackers?"

"Yes, because that's not a lie; it's just not all of the truth. Marcus doesn't need to know the program will be used only to target one person and his organization."

"I hope it works because I'm ready to fly to the Caribbean and work on my tan. And if your program doesn't work, things could get nasty very fast."

Stella gave a quick nod to her friend and said a silent prayer for God's help. If the threat wasn't eliminated soon, the entire town might be in danger.

Wilder Templeton sat back in his office chair. The interrogation had gone way too easy. The men had been more than ready to talk. The only problem was they didn't seem to know much of anything since they'd been hired off the internet. Wilder shook his head at the lack of professionalism. The guys had been promised a thousand dollars each. They were lucky they had only been tased. He shuddered at the thought of creeping around any property belonging to Stella and her friend.

Wilder could easily have his staff run traces on the IP address that contacted the men, but with Stella's computer skills, she could locate the data without any problems. However, with that scenario, he'd have to face her again.

Even though they were both in their sixties, Stella remained as attractive as ever with her silver hair and captivating green eyes. Over the years, Wilder had stayed in touch with her and her husband, but once she became a widow, he'd kept his distance to give her time to allow her heart to heal.

Maybe enough time had passed for her, but he wasn't sure he was ready to face the woman he never stopped loving.

Chapter 2

"**G**ood morning!" A young woman with long brunette hair and big brown eyes greeted Stella as she entered Knick Knacks Antique Store. "May I help you find anything?"

Stella smiled her way. "No, thank you. I'm just looking."

"If you have any questions, my name is Grace."

"Thank you, Grace. I'm Stella."

Grace came from behind the counter and walked toward her. "Oh, you must be Stella Nicely. Marcus and Olivia were telling my husband and I about you. Welcome to Crawdad Beach. I hope you like it here."

"Thank you. I am enjoying the town and the people."

Grace grinned. "It is a pretty special place."

"I'm inclined to agree with you."

The little bell over the door chimed as someone stepped inside. Grace excused herself.

The old building crowded with furniture, glassware, antique jewelry, art, old toys, and various items beckoned Stella to browse. She walked to where a stained glass sign hung over a beautiful reading nook nestled among old, massive wooden shelves filled with books and decorative objects.

Picking up a novel, Stella flipped through the pages.

Maybe someday she would write her life story. Of course, it would have to be substantially altered because no one would ever believe all she'd seen, done, and experienced. Perhaps she could make the story a novel and write under an alias. Stella chuckled under her breath. Writing under her latest assumed name would work just fine.

Taking the book, she walked to the counter where an older gentleman, his back to her, stood talking to Grace.

Grace smiled at her. "Chester Taylor, have you met Stella Nicely?"

"I don't believe I have." The white-haired gentleman turned toward Stella, and his eyes went wide.

Acting calmly, Stella quickly held her hand toward the man she'd known for years. "Nice to meet you. I just recently moved to town."

Chester's eyebrows raised, and he clasped her fingers, giving her hand a good shake. "It's nice to meet you . . . Stella." A mischievous grin spread on his face. "Welcome to Crawdad Beach. You'll have to come over for dinner sometime. I'm sure Maybelline would be glad to see you. I mean, meet you."

"That sounds lovely. We must do that soon."

"Well, I better get going." Chester turned back to Grace. "Tell your hubby I'll see him at his workshop later." He tipped an imaginary hat. "You ladies have a nice day." He grinned at Stella again as he walked past her.

Waiting until he had gone, Stella stepped to the counter. "I'd like to purchase this book, please."

"This is a good one." Grace pointed to the novel. "I read

it in one afternoon. I couldn't put it down."

"That's good to know." Stella handed the young woman cash for the purchase. "After I finish, perhaps you can tell me what other books are good to read."

"I'd love that. Escaping into an imaginary world is such fun, isn't it? You can step into a character's role and be someone different and go places and do things completely out of the ordinary."

Stella gave her a polite smile as she held up the book. "I look forward to the escape." She took her leave and stepped onto the sidewalk along the brick-paved Main Street lined with two-story brick buildings.

Besides Knick Knacks Antique Store, the town had a law office, post office, Curl and Dye Beauty Salon, Tiddlywinks Restaurant, Doohickeys Hardware, two buildings converted into loft apartments, and another undergoing renovation as a hotel.

An older couple hand-in-hand greeted her as they walked past. Two young women chatted as they pushed strollers. Stella had only been here a few weeks, yet the town made her feel welcome.

"Psst."

Stella stopped and turned toward the sound.

Standing in the front alcove of the building under renovation, Chester motioned with his hand for her to join him.

She casually walked his way.

He grabbed her arm and moved her next to him. "Did you

really move here?"

Stella chuckled. "Yes."

"Well, hot diggity dog. Maybelline will be thrilled. How long has it been?"

"Probably twenty-five years." Stella grinned at the memories of their paths crossing during her military service.

"Time sure does go by fast. So, you're going by Stella Nicely these days?"

"Yes, it made sense since I moved to such a nice little town."

"Excellent choice. So, have you retired?"

"Yes and no. I'm still working on that problem I've had for years."

Chester sucked in a breath. "No!" Gone was his playful expression, replaced with the look he often wore as a commanding officer. "Jude is still after you?"

"I'm afraid so. That's part of why I moved here."

Chester's gaze filled with concern. "You did the right thing about Jude. Don't ever regret the choice you made."

Stella's eyes filled with moisture. She'd done the right thing by turning in the man who had been selling government secrets. But, after Jude escaped capture, he had continued to torment her for decades. "I know, but it sure hasn't made my life easy."

"I'm sorry to hear this. I hoped by now Jude was in custody. Let me know if I can do anything to help." He took his phone from his back jeans pocket. "I'll text you my number." He exchanged contact information with her.

"Maybelline and I will be in prayer for you. I still have connections if you need them."

"Thank you, friend. Hopefully, the situation will soon be rectified. My friend moved here with me."

Chester tilted his head. "Your friend?" His eyes widened as realization hit him. "Oh, *that* friend. She's still in service?"

"She also retired but stays active with various projects and is still in incredible shape. Her name is now Mia Burns."

He looked over his shoulder, then leaned closer. "Mia isn't still upset with me for taking her off that mission, is she?"

"I'm not sure. It only took her a few years to remove your picture from her dart board."

Chester's tan face turned a shade lighter. "Well, let's hope she's forgiven me."

Stella chuckled. "For your sake, I hope she has."

Wilder stood at his office window. Now that he was older, he had been slowly handing the company to his vice president. He wasn't ready to fully retire, but having more time to do things he enjoyed would be nice. However, after working all these years, he wasn't sure what he really enjoyed doing.

Either way, it was time for a change, and Crawdad Beach's location might work just fine. The town was within an hour of the airport, a joint military base, and the ocean. He could keep his house and central office location, rent an apartment for a few months, and see if things progressed with Stella.

Raking his hand through his hair, Wilder sighed. Stella knew about his reputation. At one time, he'd been proud that he had dated so many women. Now, it only left him with years of regret. He couldn't change the past, but thankfully, God, in His kindness, had forgiven him. However, would Stella have anything to do with him? Maybe as a friend, but as something more?

Wilder turned to his computer and searched for rentals in Crawdad Beach. He had to convince Stella he was a new man who wanted a new beginning with her.

Chapter 3

Stella walked under the teal and white awning above the door of Rolling in the Dough Bakery, stepped inside, and breathed in the delicious, mouth-watering smells. Customers sat around bistro tables chatting and eating pastries.

The bakery walls were adorned with a mural of a cute cartoon crawdad wearing a teal apron, holding a rolling pin in one of his claws and an oven mitt in the other. An antique refurbished teal bicycle with a basket and a display cabinet of antique bakery tools hung on the other walls.

Stepping to the glass front display cases, Stella surveyed the delectable goodies and tried to decide what she would take home. Since the bakery was within walking distance, she hoped her steps would counteract some of the calories.

"Hi, Ms. Stella." Olivia Patterson's smiling face greeted her. The young woman with light brown hair and dark brown eyes was a perfect match for her friend, Marcus. With his good looks from his Latin heritage and Olivia's grandmother's Asian background, they were a handsome couple with a mutual faith.

"Hello, Olivia. Welcome back. Did you have a nice honeymoon?"

Olivia's cheeks tinged pink as her gaze turned dreamy. "It

was wonderful. That was my first time in Puerto Vallarta, and his family's villa was incredible. Of course, just being with Marcus anywhere is great." She sighed, then refocused her gaze toward her. "Are you here to buy something or see Marcus?"

As much as Stella wanted to bring Marcus up to date on what was happening, she needed to make a phone call to see how much information she could share. "I'll just buy some of your wonderful cupcakes. I'm running low on my chocolate intake."

"We mustn't allow that to happen. The double-chocolate fudge ones just came out of the oven."

"Then, I must buy six. Not all for me, of course. My roommate will probably eat a few."

Olivia placed the cupcakes in a carryout box and laid them on the counter. "Chester said that if you hold dessert high in the air, the calories will jump off."

"Well, if Chester said it, then it must be true." Stella chuckled as she paid for the purchase. "Please tell Marcus hello."

Casually surveying her surroundings, Stella walked toward her home. Even with Jude's continued attacks, she took protective precautions but trusted God for her ultimate protection. Throughout the Bible, verses reminded her not to be afraid that God was always in control. She also took comfort in the verse that said God has not given the spirit of fear but love, power, and a sound mind.

Back at her house, Stella sat in her office and munched

on a cupcake. Mia had left a note saying she would be back later this evening. There was no telling where her friend had gone this time.

Hoping the chocolate fortified her nerves, Stella finished her cupcake and placed the call. How much would Marcus's dad allow her to share with his son?

Wilder drove slowly along the main street of Crawdad Beach. When he went through town the other night, he hadn't been paying attention to anything besides getting to Stella's house. Now, in the light of day, he chuckled at the interesting and quirky names of the businesses.

He slowed to read the sign for Doohickeys Hardware. Since 1916, they proudly offered a wide range of hardware, building supplies, and whatever whatchamacallit was needed -- sounded good to him. No wonder Stella moved here.

Turning his attention back to the road, Wilder slammed on his brakes. A woman, wearing a bright red velveteen jogging suit, was hunched over the wheel of a riding lawnmower as she putted along the road. Her interesting mode of transportation even had a pink basket tied to the back of her seat.

Shaking his head, Wilder resumed his slow progress. Turning off Main Street, he passed homes of various sizes, many of which had been renovated. He stopped at the end of a cul-de-sac in front of a duplex with white shutters against a sea-green building. Each unit even had a garage.

Wilder parked in the driveway and checked his notes. The owners lived in the duplex's right side. As he walked up the sidewalk, the door opened, and a woman with sandy brown hair and eyes in her late forties gave him a pleasant smile. "You must be Wilder Templeton."

"Yes, obviously, you received my paperwork."

"We did. It's always good to have another military man in town. I'm Julie Bowman. Welcome to Crawdad Beach. My husband, Dustin, will join us in a few minutes. He's the town's mayor and also runs a software security firm. I'll show you around the unit. The apartment is fully furnished."

Wilder followed behind her as she unlocked the door and handed him the key. Stepping inside, he took in the surroundings as Julie talked about the great attributes of the town. Wilder half-listened as he checked out the open living area with light blue walls and plank wood vinyl flooring. The furnishings included a white couch, two floral chairs that thankfully weren't too foo-foo, a coffee table, and a flat-screen television that sat on a white cabinet. The rear of the room had the kitchen and dining area with French doors leading to a screened-in back porch. The bedroom and bathroom were decently sized, and the laundry area came with a washer and dryer.

Julie followed behind him. "We also include cable, Wi-fi, and a security system."

Wilder nodded. "This will work just fine. You should have received my deposit. I'll also pay for six months."

"Wonderful," Julie said. "The garage remote is on the kitchen counter. Do you know when you'll move in?"

"I brought everything with me. Looks like the place is ready to go." Wilder took out his credit card. "Moving in right now wouldn't be a problem, would it?"

"No, that would be great." She took him back to her side of the duplex to finish the paperwork and accept his payment.

Once everything was complete, Wilder returned to his place, unpacked his few belongings, and set his computer on the kitchen breakfast table. The setup for a home office wasn't ideal, but it was only temporary. He would continue driving to his main office for work.

He'd been on numerous covert missions throughout his career, but if all went well, this would be his best and finest achievement. Stella could crack almost any computer code and had single-handedly taken down criminal hackers around the world. Wilder's mission would be to find and arrest Jude and then discover the code to Stella's heart.

Chapter 4

"**F**orgive me for contacting you on your honeymoon." Stella motioned Marcus toward a chair in her office. "However, I did want you to be alert when you returned home. Thankfully, two of my friends handled last night's problem."

Behind his glasses, Marcus's gaze was curious as he sat beside her. "What's going on?"

"Your father has given me permission to brief you on a situation."

"My father?" Marcus sat straight. "You know my dad?"

"Robert is a dear friend."

Marcus's eyebrows rose momentarily. He then narrowed his brown eyes. "Wait. Did you befriend me online because you knew who I was?"

Stella gave him a slight nod. "I did have knowledge about you before we connected." Their friendship had formed through an ethical hacker group. Marcus had also helped her with several cybersecurity projects.

"I am still having a hard time since you told me who you were." Marcus cringed as he rubbed the back of his neck. "I thought Dragon-Slayer58 was my male friend and good buddy, not you." He gave her an apologetic look. "No offense."

"None taken. I never lied about who I was. I'm afraid you made some assumptions that were far from reality." Stella felt sorry for Marcus since he had assumed he was asking another man for guidance regarding the women he had dated.

"Yeah, about that. I would never have shared as many," Marcus cleared his throat, "personal things with you. And now that I know you know my dad, I'm even more uncomfortable."

Stella gave him a reassuring smile. "Your secrets are always safe with me. I prayed you would make wiser choices than when you lived in Los Angeles."

Marcus groaned. "That was an embarrassing time. Thanks for giving good advice and pointing me back to God. Enough about me. What is this situation you mentioned?"

She flicked her gaze to check her camera feeds before turning back to Marcus. "Years ago, I notified the authorities about a man named Jude Ingle who was selling government secrets. Unfortunately, he escaped capture." Stella typed on her computer keyboard, bringing up the information on Jude along with his photo on her monitors.

Marcus stood and studied the information. "I don't think I've ever seen him."

"Jude usually sends others to do his dirty work. When he hasn't tried to have me killed, he has worked at ways to make my life miserable. Before you were born, your father and I were on a mission together. The internet wasn't widely used then, and we needed to be physically present at a location. Unfortunately, that was when Jude made one of his attempts on my life. Your father bravely pushed me aside and took a bullet in his shoulder."

Marcus sat again in his chair and blew out a breath. "Dad never told me about that. When I was a kid, he always made light of his scars, saying he had fought off a dinosaur, rhinoceros or was attacked by baby sharks. Once I got older, I could tell they were bullet and knife wounds."

"Robert is a humble man who has received many medals."

Marcus's eyebrows raised to his hairline. "I'm surprised I've never seen any of his awards. Wow, the more I learn about Dad, the more I love and admire him."

"It's the same way with our heavenly Father." The more she learned about God, the more her love for Him grew.

Marcus nodded. "That's true. I like that thought. So, what about your dad? Was he military?"

Tamping down any wayward emotions, Stella surveyed her wall of computer screens while she tried to formulate a response. "I never knew my parents. As a newborn, I was left at an orphanage."

His gaze filled with concern. "I'm sorry. I shouldn't have asked."

"Don't worry. I wouldn't want to relive my childhood. However, through that time, I learned to rely on God, my ever-present Father." Stella hadn't been abused as a child but was rarely given attention or love. Thankfully, she had found comfort in a relationship with God. She turned her attention back to Marcus. "Enough about me. Back to the situation at hand. Jude's anger toward me has grown to include others.

Especially those he knows I am fond of. Benjamin, my late husband's death was listed as a heart attack, but I believe Jude may have been behind my husband's demise."

Marcus cringed. "Man, I'm sorry. That's not good. Did you tell the police or someone in the government?"

"There are those who know of my situation," Stella said.

"So, how can I help? And, besides my father being involved at some point, what does this have to do with me?"

"Although I've told you the software you and I are developing is a security package, it will mainly be used to track Jude. Last fall, when you sought my help because hackers demanded money from you, I noticed a line of code. Jude knows my computer skills and left his calling card in the malicious software. That's why I moved to Crawdad Beach. You thought your past had returned to haunt you, but I'm afraid you are also now in Jude's crosshairs."

Marcus pushed out of his chair and paced back and forth. "I just got married. I can't let anything happen to Olivia."

"We are keeping an eye on you both." Stella typed on her computer keyboard and pointed to two of her screens on her wall. The feed from the building where Marcus and Olivia lived came online.

He shot her a look. "You're watching us?"

"Not your private quarters. Just the feed from the front and back of the bakery. We are also monitoring your security system. "

"We?"

"Me, my friends Mia and Wilder, and your father are

keeping watch."

Marcus ran his hand through his brown hair, leaving it in disarray. "I don't know whether to be grateful or freak out."

"Marcus, you've never been out of your father's loving care."

He slumped in his chair and stared at her. "That is the most comforting yet disturbing news I've ever received."

"You have nothing to worry about. No matter where you've gone or what you've done, your father's love never changed. Now, let's get to work and finish that software and see if we can't put an end to Jude's torment of us all."

The wood floors creaked as Wilder entered Doohickeys Hardware Store. Deep, rich wood shelving that looked original contained items that seemed to have been there for years, while others looked brand new.

Wilder stopped in front of a wooden whatchamacallit box and peered inside. He'd never seen so many unique items in all his life. Old bolts, nails, screws, metal clasps, hinges, along with other items that he had no clue what they were.

"May I help you?" A man, approximately forty-five, six-foot tall with black hair with a touch of grey around his temples and blue eyes, stood beside him.

"Just checking out the whatchamacallits."

"Feel free to take anything you might need. We've kept the tradition going since the store opened. I'm Doohickeys owner, Eric Reed." He held out his hand.

Wilder shook it. "Thanks. Wilder Templeton."

"You here visiting?"

"I'm renting a place for a few months."

"In the loft apartments here in downtown?"

"No, a duplex." Wilder glanced at the display cabinet on the back wall filled with antique hardware items.

"Oh, you're renting the unit next to the Bowmans. Welcome to Crawdad Beach. What brings you here?"

Wilder considered how much to share with the man. "I thought I'd see what living in a small town would be like."

"In my opinion, this is the best place on earth."

"Good to know."

"We'll be closing soon. Since it's almost dinner time, make sure you try Tiddlywinks restaurant. They have the best food in town."

Wilder bit back a grin. As far as he knew, that was the only place to eat in Crawdad Beach.

"Don't miss stopping by tomorrow morning at Rolling in the Dough," Eric continued. "Best pastries anywhere."

"Don't let him fool you. His stepdaughter owns the bakery."

Wilder turned toward the voice and grinned. "Chester Taylor, what are you doing here."

His old friend walked up and smacked him on the back. "I live here. The bakery is great, by the way. What are *you* doing here?"

"Just renting a place for a little while."

"He's over at the Bowman's duplex," Eric said.

Chester gave a nod. "Nice place." He studied Wilder for a moment, then his eyebrow raised. "Oh, I just figured out why you're here. It wouldn't have anything to do with a lady we both know, would it?"

Wilder tried to act calm, cool, and collected. But, under Chester's scrutiny, heat rose up his back. "I will neither confirm nor deny your question."

Chester bopped him on the arm. "You old dog, you. I would never put you two together."

Eric gazed back and forth between them. "Am I missing something?"

"No," Chester said as he waved his hand. "Me and Wilder go way back. I'm just giving him a hard time."

"Well, let me know if either of you need anything."

As Eric walked away, Wilder grabbed Chester's arm and moved close. "I would prefer my connection to Stella to stay quiet."

"She doesn't know you're interested or that you're here?"

"Both," Wilder growled.

Chester chuckled. "Well, things around here might be getting interesting. Need my help?"

"No." Wilder released his arm and stepped back. "If I'm going to mess this up, I'd prefer to do it on my own."

"Okay, fine." Chester, still smiling, shook his head. "But it is good to see you. How have you been?"

"Good. Much better than before. My life has changed." How grateful Wilder was for God's grace. Especially in his case.

"Changed, huh?" Chester narrowed his eyes as he surveyed him. "I see it now. You don't have that Wilder, wild-eyed look anymore."

"Let's just say I'm finally heading in the right direction."

"Well, I'll be. You get saved?"

Wilder nodded. "In the most extreme way. God got my attention."

Chester whistled. "With you, that must have been a doozy. Did God zap you with a lightning bolt?"

"Almost. Let's just say getting shot in the back woke me up. Especially when I could hear the medical team saying I was too far gone." Wilder shuddered. He'd been shot before, but he'd never come that close to dying.

"Whew, that must have been rough to hear."

"Definitely. I knew if I was too far gone, I would not be going to a good place."

"Good thing you pulled through."

"Yes, I will be eternally grateful." Wilder pointed up as he said a silent prayer of thanks to God.

"Well, you just made my day. Do you want to come over for dinner tonight? I'm sure Maybelline would love to see you."

"If you tell her I've changed, she'll want to see me. Otherwise, she might hit me with a frying pan."

Chester's eyes crinkled with his smile. "Yeah, you left quite an impression on her the last time she saw you. But I don't think she ever gave up praying for you."

Wilder breathed a silent prayer of thanks. "Tell her I am grateful that she and God didn't give up on me."

Chapter 5

After saying goodbye to Marcus, Stella locked the door, set her alarm, and returned to her office. They had made significant headway on the software program, but he needed to get home and spend time with his new wife.

Stella sighed at the sweet memory of her marriage. Her love for Benjamin had changed, grown, and deepened over the years. He would always be missed. They had such a nice life together in Maryland. Not that they had done anything with other couples; they kept mainly to themselves.

She never intended to move, but after praying for months, she felt the prompting to sell her home and relocate to Crawdad Beach. Part of the reason was probably to be closer to Marcus and keep an eye on him, yet she felt God had something else in store for her. Even though she could retire, she planned to continue working in cybersecurity. Every day brought unique challenges that kept her mind sharp and her day busy.

Movement on her backyard camera feed focused Stella's attention. Mia was home. The alarm beeped as she entered the code, stepped inside, and reset the alarm again. A few minutes later, Mia, wearing a very stylish dress that hugged her curves, stepped into Stella's office.

Mia checked the computer monitors before turning toward her. “So, did I miss anything exciting?”

“No. All’s been quiet. What have you been up to?”

Mia gave her a look. “You don’t want to know.”

“No. Probably not.” With her friend, there was no telling where she’d been. With her skills in martial arts, archery, knife-throwing, and shooting, Stella was grateful they were good friends and on good terms. “Oh, I did run into an old acquaintance of ours. Chester Taylor.”

Mia raised an eyebrow. “Interesting. He lives here?”

“He does and is still married to Maybelline. He was rather worried when I mentioned you lived here with me.”

Mia chuckled. “I bet he is. Lucky for him, I don’t have any hard feelings, but I sure don’t mind him squirming and wondering.”

“He invited me to have dinner with them sometime.”

“Chester didn’t invite me? I’m crushed.” Mia laid a hand on her forehead and acted like she was swooning.

“Oh, please, as though you would be upset. But if you are, I could text him to see if it would be okay for you to join us.”

“No.” Mia gave a throaty laugh. “I’d much rather find him in the wild and surprise him. Well, I better get ready. I have a date this evening.”

Stella followed her down the hall. “Anyone I know?”

“No. He’s mine, all mine. Forever and ever.” Mia never had difficulty finding suitors. It would be nice if her friend could find someone to love and be loved in a long-term marriage relationship.

"That sounds interesting and promising. Have you known him long?"

Mia's grin was mischievous. "Long enough." Her expression turned more serious. "I think it's time for you to consider love again."

"Me? Why on earth would I do that?" Stella shook her head. She'd had her chance; her time with Benjamin had been wonderful. No, she didn't need to consider that option.

"Maybe you should be open if God has someone else planned for your future?"

"I doubt that.

Mia stepped closer. "For someone who loves God, why do you shortchange that He might have something good for your future?" With that, she entered her portion of the house and shut the door.

Stella walked back to her office, sat in her chair, and stared at the screens on the wall before her. She'd had her one chance at love. Before her marriage, she'd made it on her own, and she could do it again.

Once again, it would be her and God, and that would be enough.

Wilder sat at his computer and checked his list. So far, he'd stopped by every business downtown and familiarized himself with each street in Crawdad Beach. He also introduced himself to the silver-haired Police Chief Weaver and the other officer, the over six foot, blonde, blue-eyed man named Gabriel.

Wilder had given them his business card, which had the name of his well-known security company. He wasn't taking any chances if he was spotted walking around the area or lingering around Stella's house. He'd been discreet in what he shared with the officers, but they needed to know there was a threat against her life.

Wilder found it interesting how the men seemed to take the news in stride, telling him they had dealt with that kind of situation before and even exchanged cell phone numbers with him. Wilder rubbed the back of his neck.

Just what was going on behind the scenes in what looked like such a sleepy little town with a cartoon crawdad for a mascot?

Chapter 6

Holding the bakery sack filled with still-warm pastries, Stella couldn't wait to return home and enjoy the delectable treats. Of course, she might share a few with Mia.

On the sidewalk coming toward her, a silver-haired gentleman with a little black and white dog stopped in front of her. The man smiled and held out his hand. "Hello. You must be new here. I'm Henry Doss." The man smelled of soap and sunshine. Although she'd never met him, the man seemed, in a strange way, oddly familiar.

She shook his outstretched hand. "Hello, Henry. I'm Stella Nicely."

"Stella, it's nice to meet you. Chester mentioned that he was happy you had moved here. Welcome to Crawdad Beach." Henry pointed to the dog now sitting at his feet. "This is Filbert."

She patted the little pup's furry head. The cute animal wagged his tail and looked like he even smiled.

Henry pointed to the bag she was carrying. "You must have picked up some pastries from Rolling in the Dough. My granddaughter, Olivia Baker, is the owner. I mean Olivia Patterson."

"Oh, yes, she married Marcus. She seems like such a

sweet young lady."

Henry's smile deepened. "Yes, she is. Thank you." He tilted his head as his piercing, radiant blue eyes gazed at her. "Forgive me for staring. You have the most striking green eyes. My mother had eyes like yours. Fascinating. I've never seen anyone else with that eye color. Did you inherit them from someone in your family?"

Surprised at his questions, Stella shrugged. "I'm not sure. I was dropped off at an orphanage hours after I was born." She rarely shared that fact with others, yet for some reason, Henry made her feel welcome and comfortable.

His eyes held compassion. "I'm terribly sorry to hear that. My mother abandoned me when I was four. She said she was going to the store and never returned."

Stella stood there, not sure how to respond. Should she apologize for having the same eye color as his mother? From the peaceful look on his face, Stella would never have thought he had a bad day in his life. "I'm sorry."

"Yes, it was difficult. Yet, God took care of me."

Stella relaxed. She would be forever grateful for God's presence in her own life. "God is good about that, isn't He?"

Henry nodded. "Yes, and when we are His, we are brought into His family. Perhaps you would like to join us at church on Sunday? It's the white-steepled building when you first drive into town. We would love to have you with us."

"Thank you for the invitation." When Benjamin was alive, they went to church together but didn't get involved; they just listened to the sermon and went home. Attending a service with people she saw around Crawdad Beach would be nice. "Maybe I can come."

"Excellent. I hope to see you there." Henry walked away with Filbert, staying in step with him.

Stella returned home, fixed herself a cup of coffee, and placed a crawdad claw on her plate. She chuckled at the creative name of the bakery's version of the pastry, usually called a bear claw.

"Good morning." Wearing a cute top and slacks, Mia came into the kitchen and looked in the bakery sack. "What did you bring me?"

"A crawdad claw."

Mia's nose wrinkled. "I do not think I would want that for breakfast."

Stella grinned. "It's just a cute name for the pastry. This is Crawdad Beach, you know."

"True. This town does have a quirky sense of humor." Mia made herself a cup of coffee, got a pastry, and sat across from her at the table. "So, what's on your agenda today?"

Stella took a bite of the yummy pastry and sighed. Good thing she was at least getting some exercise by walking. "Marcus and I are finishing the software package, and I have another project waiting in the wings. How about you?"

"I will be spending time with my man." Mia munched on her crawdad claw.

"Sounds like it's getting serious. Will I meet said man at any time? Or do I already know him? Perhaps a mutual friend?"

"You've met him."

"Really? Someone I know?" Stella's brain rifled through the men who might be Mia's love interest. Several came to mind, but one jumped to the forefront. "Wilder, maybe?"

"No, he has his sights on another woman."

"Do I know who that might be?"

Mia nodded and grinned like she knew something more than she was telling. "Oh, yes, you know her quite well."

"That sounds interesting." Again, Stella's brain tried to think of who Wilder might be interested in. She'd heard he had changed and become a Christian, but at one time, he dated most of the single women she knew. "Are you going to give me a hint?"

"Nope. You are on your own. Maybe you can ask him."

"Ask him? I don't see him anymore."

"You need to open your eyes. Wilder is here in Crawdad Beach."

"What? What's he doing here?"A warm fuzzy feeling enveloped Stella. She hadn't realized how much she missed him.

Mia raised an eyebrow. "You don't have a clue, do you? He's here to try and keep you safe."

"That's very nice of him, but I'm fine. We can handle things."

Mia growled and slapped the table. "Jude has been making your life miserable for decades. It's time to end this. You've gotten used to Jude doing something and then leaving you alone for a while. You're assuming you don't have to worry for a month or two, but you need to have a life."

Why was her friend getting so angry? Stella held up her hands. "I have a life. I'm fine. God takes care of me."

"I know that. I know you try not to live in fear, trust God, and rely on Him, but let your friends help put a stop to Jude."

"I appreciate your help and Wilder's help, but I'll be fine."

Mia blew out a breath and shook her head. "That's your typical answer. I'll be fine. I've known you for decades, and you're still a closed book."

Stella sat straight. "What do you mean?"

"There's a difference between relying on God and being open to how God might work. I know you made it at the orphanage on your own, and you and Benjamin had a good life together, but you don't do anything other than work and stay home. You've kept your life closed off. We're friends, but you even keep me at arm's length."

Stella crossed her arms over her chest, then put her arms back down. "I do not."

"Seriously? What I just said about your life is basically all I know about your life."

"I probably don't know that much about you either." Stella hated she sounded so argumentative.

"You know much more about me. Because every time we've had a personal conversation, you switch the attention off you and back on me."

"That's because I'm interested in what happens with you. You're my friend."

"Yes, and I will always be your friend. But I'm not going

to be here much longer. I'll be alive, God willing, but I have plans that don't include being your roommate."

"I know that. I know this is only temporary. I'll be fine." Stella got to her feet and went to make a cup of coffee. She hated getting personal.

"There you go again. No matter what happens, you say you'll be fine."

Stella tried to temper her growing anger. "It's true. I'll be fine."

"God's got you. I get that. But, sometimes, God sends people to be part of His plan. I'm here because I believe God wants me to help you before I move on. Wilder feels the same way. I don't know if you have trust issues or are just too prideful to reach out for help."

Stella turned away. She hated the moisture building in her eyes. She hated crying or showing emotion and hated needing anyone because when she was a little girl, she desperately needed someone, anyone, to love and care for her. God had been the only one who cared.

Mia's arm came around her shoulder. "Sometimes trusting God means letting go of how we think things will work so we don't get in God's way in how *He* wants to work. Let us help you. Wilder and his team are trying to locate Jude. You and Marcus are developing a program. I also have something in the works. We're getting close. Let your friends, who love you, help you."

Stella clenched her fists and willed herself to stop feeling. She appreciated her friends wanting to help, but still, whatever came next, she'd be fine—just her and God. Like always.

Chapter 7

Wilder's team had spotted Jude leaving the Fayetteville airport. Disconnecting the call, Wilder checked the time. Nine thirty. At this time of night, if Jude was heading to Crawdad Beach, they had over an hour to intercept him.

Wilder sent a quick message to Mia. She responded that she wasn't with Stella but would be there within the hour. *Blast it, where was she?* Stella didn't need to be alone. Sending up a quick prayer, Wilder grabbed his keys and drove to her house.

Walking up the steps, Wilder nodded toward the security camera and waited on the front stoop under the porch light. He took a deep breath, stood tall, hoped he was presentable. He'd seen Stella from a distance plenty of times, but it had been over a year since she'd seen him. He needed to convince her that he no longer lived up to his Wilder name and was a changed man.

The door opened, and Stella, her silver hair pulled back in a ponytail, gazed up at him with her captivating green eyes. "Wilder Templeton, it's good to see you. Won't you come in?" She stepped aside to let him enter, locked the door behind him, and motioned toward her couch. "Can I get you anything?"

"No, thank you." He didn't sit; he just stood there. Stella didn't even give him a welcome hug or seem surprised that he was at her house. He tried not to let his shoulders droop. "I'm here because Jude may be on his way."

Stella raised an eyebrow, but her expression remained neutral. "Well, I better get ready. Follow me." She walked down a hall, stopped at the door, punched in a code, and stepped inside. A bank of monitors on the wall included video from camera security feeds around her house, the bakery, and others had data scrolling like he'd seen at many government facilities.

He nodded toward her setup. "Looks like you're staying busy."

"Always. Boredom is not something I enjoy." Stella crossed to a bookcase filled with books and documents. On her tiptoes, she tugged on the book titled *War and Peace*. The bookcase swung open, revealing an impressive stash of weapons. "The hiding place may be a bit cliché, but it works. Mia's connections helped us take care of the security protocols for my home."

Wilder bit back a grin and stepped closer. "I guess I didn't need to worry about you."

Stella gave him a wry smile. "I may rely on God, but that doesn't mean I'm unprepared."

"I'm glad to hear that on both of those counts."

"I had heard you had some life changes." She tilted her head, her gaze intense. "Your eyes do look different."

Wilder tried not to widen his eyes. "I hope they show my

heart change. I thank God, but I wish I could thank Benjamin. He never gave up on me."

"No, he didn't. Benjamin always prayed that you would receive Christ as Savior. I prayed for you, too," Stella said.

"Thank you. It took a bullet to open my eyes, but it was worth it. I just wish I had become a Christian much sooner."

"It's not an easy life, but it is the best life for now and all eternity."

He smiled and nodded. "I agree."

She closed her hidden room. "I assume you came prepared?"

Wilder patted his holstered gun. "Always."

"Could I get you something to drink? I have water, iced tea, or lemonade."

"No, I'm good. Thanks."

"We can wait in here, then." She motioned to one of the chairs at the desk in front of her monitors.

Once she took a seat, Wilder sat next to her. "How have you been, Stella?"

Her smile seemed somewhat forced. "I'm fine. I miss Benjamin, but I'm making a new life here."

"So you think you'll stay in Crawdad Beach?"

"I do. After Benjamin passed, I prayed about what I needed to do next, and here I am." Stella's gaze moved to her screens for a moment before turning back to him. "How about you? Mia mentioned you were living here. Is that just temporary?"

He shrugged. "It depends."

Stella studied him and then grinned. "I had heard you were interested in someone. Does she live in the area?"

"Yes, she does."

"I hope to meet her sometime."

"I'm sure you will." Enjoying sitting with the woman who had his full interest, Wilder relaxed.

"Is she a nice lady? A Christian?"

"Yes, on both counts, but I don't think she has any idea how special she is."

Stella's smile was genuine. "Oh, Wilder, I hope you have found the woman of your dreams. The one God has for you."

He leaned toward her. "I believe I have."

"That makes me happy. You've been a wandering soul for many years."

"Yes, for far too long." Wilder tried not to show his disappointment that Stella's excitement was because she thought he was interested in another woman. Her otherwise friendly and polite reactions showed absolutely no interest in him other than a friend. Why had he thought she would welcome him with open arms?

In the back of his mind, a song from the 1970s played about what a fool believed about a relationship that had no chance.

Stella turned to survey her video and computer screens. She had missed Wilder. Why had he disappeared after

Benjamin's death? Perhaps Wilder was dealing with his grief in his own way, or maybe he had been dating the woman he was interested in.

The thought that Wilder may have found someone he was serious about pleased her and yet made her a little sad, which didn't make sense. He had always been handsome, but now his looks were even more attractive. She shook off the thought since she wasn't looking for a relationship. God had given her a good man to marry, and that time was over. She needed a subject change. "Did you know Chester lives in town?"

Wilder nodded. "I did. I ran into him. He and Maybelline live behind the duplex where I'm staying."

"That's too funny. Who would have thought we would all live in the same place."

"Makes you wonder who else might be in the area." His gaze flicked to her monitors. "Let's just hope Jude isn't heading this way."

"To be honest, I have mixed emotions," Stella said. "I'm ready to end Jude's activities. I mean, not end, end. Just turn him over to the authorities. It would be nice not always to wonder what he will do next."

Wilder's jaw clenched momentarily. "It stinks that it's gone this long. Jude should have been captured decades ago. It makes me wonder who has been protecting him."

"I had wondered the same thing." The thought made her skin crawl that someone might be protecting him. "I knew he often used hired help, but you think someone else is involved?"

"I don't know, but anything is possible. I'm sorry I wasn't more help to you over the years. But I didn't know until recently that you were still having problems with Jude."

Maybe what Mia said was true. Avoiding Wilder's gaze, Stella turned her attention to her screens. Had she kept her life so closed off that she hadn't even shared her problems with those who were her friends? Stella hadn't even let Benjamin tell anyone. By keeping the situation to herself, had she inadvertently endangered the lives of others? What if Jude had flown into the area not only to harm her but Marcus?

Stella turned her gaze to the bakery's video feeds as an unsettled feeling came over her. "Wilder, can I hire your security firm to watch over someone else for me?"

"Sure. Just let me know who and when."

"Right now, please. Call someone on your team. I need you to keep Marcus Patterson and his wife, Olivia, safe for me. They live in the bakery building downtown." The urgency growing by the second, Stella stood. "Please, call now!"

Chapter 8

Surprised at Stella's strong reaction, Wilder placed the call and ensured he had a team to cover her house and the bakery building.

Even though her gaze never left the security camera feeds, Stella paced back and forth.

Wilder stood and kept in step with her. "Why are you worried about a couple who own a bakery?"

"Marcus Patterson is Robert Patterson's son," Stella said that as though everything should make sense.

Wilder wanted to shrug, but from the look on her face, he didn't. Robert had worked with him several times—a nice man and a hero on many missions. But why would Jude have an interest in Robert or Marcus? "Okay, that's interesting, but why would that matter?"

"Robert was wounded in the shoulder when he protected me from one of Jude's attacks. Robert's wife was pregnant with Marcus then, and I've always felt terrible that Robert could have been killed because of me. So, I've kept an eye on Marcus throughout the years."

Some of the pieces started falling into place. "So, you think Jude will try to harm Marcus because of your affection for him?"

"Yes, I do." She stopped pacing and faced him. "And there's something else. I believe Jude was behind Benjamin's death."

Wilder's stomach dropped. "What? I thought Ben died of a heart attack."

"He did, but Benjamin had a full physical, including heart tests, only a few weeks before his death and was given a clean bill of health. However, the autopsy showed major heart damage."

"Why wasn't there an investigation?"

"There was a hurried examination into Benjamin's death that was quickly dismissed and was not detailed."

Wilder's blood boiled. He had thought something else was going on. Now, he knew. "With your cybersecurity skills, have you found anything to trace who else might be involved?"

"I have my suspicions."

"Do you want to give me some names?"

She squeezed her eyes shut and took a shuddering breath before returning his gaze. "I'm not sure that would be wise. What might be going on behind the scenes is extremely disturbing." A flash of vulnerability flashed in Stella's eyes. "It worries me that you're here and involved with what is happening in my life. I've kept silent over the years because the more I've discovered, the more I realize there are few people I can trust."

"You aren't alone." With a cautious and careful touch, he wrapped his arms around her. Her body was tense, and her arms remained by her side, but he didn't let her go. "I'm here, and I'm not going anywhere."

Embraced in Wilder's gentle but strong arms, Stella squeezed her eyes shut to keep her tears from falling. As much as it felt good to be near him, why would he care and risk being put in danger? Maybe because he'd been Benjamin's friend. But still, she sensed there was something more, something in the way Wilder looked at her. But why would he see her any other way but a friend?

Oh, she didn't know what to do. She wanted to stay close but wanted to push away. Against her better judgment, Stella put her arms around him and laid her head against his chest. For now, maybe just this once, she would let her heart beat again.

"What's going on in here?" Mia, with a mischievous grin and eyebrows raised, stood in the doorway.

Stella stepped away from Wilder as she straightened her shirt, which didn't need straightening. She couldn't believe she hadn't noticed Mia on the camera security feed or heard the alarm beep and reset.

Wilder cleared his throat and rubbed the back of his neck. "We were just discussing the case."

"Well, don't let me interrupt your discussion," Mia said as she pointed behind them. "But you might want to look at the bakery camera feed."

Stella jerked her attention to the screen and moved closer to look. Her heart rammed into her throat. Two figures moved toward the back door in the semi-darkness behind the bakery building. "We need to get over there!"

Mia stopped her and motioned with her chin. "Keep watching."

The video feed went dark.

Stella wanted to get in her arsenal and run downtown. But then the screen reset and came online again. The area was now clear. "What happened?"

Mia grinned as she glanced at Wilder. "His team took care of things. I ran into them as I came into town."

"I'll let you know what I find out." Wilder moved toward the door, then stopped, his gaze serious. "You two stay here, keep watch, and make sure your alarm stays on. If one of them wasn't Jude, he's still out there."

"I'll let you out." Mia followed him out the door.

Stella sat in her chair and stared at the screens. She should have been watching instead of hugging Wilder. She would never forgive herself if something happened to Marcus and Olivia.

A few minutes later, the alarm beeped, and she watched as Marcus stepped outside and left in his car.

Mia came back in and propped her ridiculously firm backside on the desk. "Want to tell me what you two were doing?"

"Nothing. We weren't doing anything." Stella avoided looking at her friend. "Wilder just wanted me to know I wasn't alone."

Mia didn't say anything for a few moments. "You do know he's in love with you."

"What? No! We're just friends. He's interested in another woman."

Mia scoffed. "You and Benjamin were Wilder's friend, but he's always loved you."

Stella drew back. "That's ridiculous." Surely that wasn't true. They had been friends for decades. Wilder had even introduced Benjamin to her.

"Why do you think Wilder never married?"

Stella waved a hand in her friend's direction. "Stop, you're just making up things in your head. Wilder said he's found someone, and it sounds serious."

Mia got in her face. "That someone is you."

Chapter 9

Five o'clock in the morning, Stella sat at the kitchen table and sipped her coffee. Even though Mia had taken over watching the security feeds in the early morning hours, Stella hadn't slept for tossing and turning in bed. She was worried about Marcus and Olivia, worried that something almost happened to that sweet couple, and worried that something could happen to Mia or Wilder.

In her head, Stella recited several Bible verses on not being afraid and trusting God. She shuddered at the memory she wished she could forget of Jude's evil dark eyes. As charming as Jude was with others, she had sensed something evil lurking within him. Yet, she had pushed aside her concerns and listened to those who said Jude was a good guy. Good? The man was pure evil. Why did she listen to Lorraine Moreno? Even if Lorraine was higher up in the chain of command, it didn't mean she was correct in her positive assessment of Jude.

Stella groaned. Why didn't she pay attention to her concerns about Jude and push back on him being hired to their team? Why couldn't she go back in time and fix everything? Wanting to scream, Stella raked her hands through her hair.

Why hadn't she reached out sooner to Wilder for help? For crying out loud, he owned a security company. Maybe he could have stopped Jude years ago. Benjamin had begged her to tell Wilder, but Stella had refused, not wanting to bother their friend. *Friend.* Is that all Wilder was? A friend? Why didn't she know he cared for her? Was what Mia said true that Wilder loved her? How could he?

Stella had known Wilder before Benjamin, but Wilder never asked her out on a date. Not that she probably would have said yes since he already had a reputation as a ladies' man. Still, Wilder had always treated her with kindness. When Benjamin asked Stella to date him, she'd accepted without another look. Had she misjudged Wilder and how he saw her all those years ago?

She walked to the sink and threw the remainder of her tepid coffee down the drain. She couldn't go back and change the past. Benjamin had been a wonderful husband, and Stella didn't regret their time together. Although she did wish she had children. But they had waited while she was active in covert missions, and then time just got away from them.

Mia, wearing cute Capri leggings and a tank top, jogged into the room. "I'm going on a run. You okay?"

"Sure, I'm fine."

Her friend stood next to her and narrowed her eyes. "You look like heck."

"Thanks. You know how to make someone feel better."

"Hey, I know it's been hard, but we'll get Jude. He's not going to get away this time." Mia nudged her. "Today is a new day, and Jude usually doesn't do anything in daylight. The evil man loves hiding in the darkness. Plus, Wilder will make sure Marcus, Olivia, and you stay safe. Did you read Wilder's text this morning? We were both on the update."

Stella shook her head. "No. Did he send something? I left my phone in the bedroom."

"Well, go and get it, and get yourself cleaned up. You might have a visitor soon." Mia turned off the alarm and stepped outside. "I'll see you later." The door closed behind her, and the alarm reset.

Curious, Stella went to her bedroom and checked her phone to read Wilder's text. Her stomach churned at what Jude's men had planned. Thanking God that they had been stopped, Stella checked the next message. Marcus's dad, Robert, and his team were on the way.

Crawdad Beach would soon be crawling with covert operatives. Maybe this time, Jude would be caught.

Eating the best cinnamon roll he'd ever eaten, Wilder sat in the bakery and casually watched customers enter and exit the business. He'd already scoped out the place, making sure he knew where the exits were located and any areas that might need to be watched closer.

At the table on his left, a young woman from his team took a sip of coffee before typing on her laptop. Her cover as a writer should keep anyone from being suspicious about her presence for the next three hours. Another member of the team would take the afternoon shift.

Wilder rubbed his forehead, trying to get rid of the pounding in his head. Last night, he'd spent hours interrogating the men his team had picked up outside the bakery. Once again, Jude had hired men off the internet, promising them two thousand dollars if they broke into the bakery and attacked Marcus. Jude had left it open for the men to do whatever they wanted if Olivia was there. Wilder tried to keep his anger under control. His jaw clenched so hard his teeth screamed in protest. They had to find Jude.

Wilder had already added additional security details for 24/7 surveillance of Stella, Marcus, and his wife, Olivia. He'd also called Marcus's dad, Robert, to let him know what was happening.

The bell over the front door dinged, and a postman carrying a leather pouch walked to the counter. "I have a package for Marcus Baker. The man, about six feet tall with brown hair, handed Olivia a cardboard paper-wrapped box.

"Thank you," she said. "Do I need to sign anything?"

The man shrugged. "No."

Olivia tilted her head. "I haven't seen you before."

He looked away. "Just started today."

"Oh, welcome to Crawdad Beach."

"Thanks." He turned and left.

Wilder got to his feet, tapped his team member's table to ensure she was watching, and hurried toward Olivia. "Would you mind if I see the package?"

"My package?" Olivia gave him a curious glance as she stepped back and tightened her grip on the parcel.

Wilder mentally smacked himself in the head. Maybe he should have introduced himself. He gave her a pleasant smile. "I'm a friend of Stella's."

Olivia's eyes widened. "Oh, okay." She handed it to him.

Wilder took one look, and he knew.

Package in hand, he ran toward the back door and called over his shoulder. "Call 911!"

Chapter 10

Boom!

Wilder glared at the copy the police had given him of the typed note and the photo of the stupid windup alarm found in the package. The town was now crawling with government and security personnel. Jude probably wouldn't try anything else, at least not today.

Fortunately, Wilder's team had captured the fake postman and taken him before anyone else picked him up. They discovered that Jude had hired the man off the internet and sent him the postman clothing, leather bag, package, and a thousand dollars to deliver the parcel. The clueless delivery guy had thought it was a big joke and had no idea what trouble he had gotten into.

Jude had tormented Stella for decades. Why hadn't anyone caught the man? Wilder slammed his hand on his desk. With all of today's technology, tracking Jude shouldn't be hard for the government, Stella, or Wilder's security team. There had to be more going on behind the scenes.

Wilder placed a call to Robert. They needed to sit down and find out what exactly had happened thirty years ago and who else had been on that team.

Stella had prayed about a million thank-you prayers to God that the bomb had been a fake. What if it had been real and Wilder hadn't been at the bakery and noticed the man posing as a postman? What if Olivia or Marcus had opened the package and it had really been a bomb? How many people might have been injured or died?

Sitting in her office desk chair, she watched the camera feeds of the bakery and her house. This was all her fault. She should never have moved to Crawdad Beach and endangered so many people. Thirty years ago, Robert had been shot because of her, and now his son was in danger. Stella pressed against the bridge of her nose to stop her tears. Why had she even been born?

An arm came around her shoulder. "This is not your fault." She hadn't even heard Mia come into the office.

As comforting as her friend's words were, Stella shook her head. "You know as well as I do this would never have happened if I hadn't been here."

Mia sat in the chair next to her. "You are not responsible for the evil actions of Jude Ingle."

"I should just leave. Go live on a deserted island, so no one else gets hurt."

"Oh, good grief. Stop trying to be a martyr and all dramatic. Get over your pity party, and let's find Jude before he hurts anyone else." Mia stood and pulled Stella to her feet.

"You're always talking about trusting God and not living in fear, so start walking like you've been talking."

Stella stared at her friend. She was right. It was time to get moving. Jude was still out there, and it was time to stop the man and his evil activities. She needed to ramp up her cyber skills.

Four and a half hours later, Stella squinted at one of her computer screens. Could this be the answer she was looking for? Praying it would work, she typed in the code and pressed send. Now, they would wait and see if it worked.

A text popped on her phone.

You're still trying to trace me? Stella, the more people you bring into my game the more will die.

See you soon, Jude.

Chapter 11

"**S**it down; you're wearing a hole in the floor." Wilder waited until Mia semi-settled in a chair in his makeshift office at his kitchen table. Anger and anxiety seemed to ooze from her every pore. He understood how she felt. His adrenaline was pumping, and he was about to jump out of his skin.

"Why didn't anyone know this before now?" Mia shot him a glare. "We should have known Jude had help."

Wilder grimaced and nodded. He had suspicions but hadn't been sure before now who was protecting Jude. "When I talked to Robert, we compared notes, and everything became clear. But we can't keep beating ourselves up for not figuring this out sooner. If we don't tread carefully, this knowledge could put us all in danger from more than Jude."

Mia got back to her feet. "You want to trust people, especially those on missions with you and those higher up in the chain of command. I never suspected, never once thought about the connection they had with Jude. How could I not have seen that? I'm so mad I could spit."

Despite what they were discussing, Wilder bit back a grin. Mia's skills were deadly. "I would have thought you would have a stronger sentiment."

She narrowed her eyes into slits. "You know what I

mean."

Grateful Mia was on their side, Wilder squirmed and adjusted his seat slightly farther away from where she stood. "Marcus and Olivia have been placed in protective custody, and Robert and his team have taken over running the bakery. We don't think Jude will try again at that location, but we wanted to ensure the young couple were safe."

"I know your people are watching Stella's house, but I need to get back and stay inside with her."

"I agree." Wilder walked her to the door. "Be careful."

After locking up, he checked the time. Eight thirty at night. So far, things stayed quiet. What would Jude try next? His attacks were usually months apart and varied from irritating to deadly, but now they were coming in rapid fire.

How had Stella been able to function all these years? She'd always seemed calm and controlled, as though nothing worried her. If he didn't know her better, he would have thought she was completely delusional. But Stella's faith was paramount in her life. Even Benjamin had been impressed and amazed at how she could face any problem and weather any storm with grace. All Wilder wanted to do was find Jude and beat him senseless before turning him over to the authorities.

Wilder groaned; that probably wasn't exactly the proper Christian response. Then again, he could read some of David's Psalms, where David asked God to take extreme action against wicked people. Maybe God would understand his own anger.

A pounding on his front door sent Wilder's pulse racing.

Was Mia back? Had something happened? He ran to the door and, without checking to see who might be there, threw it open.

Chester shoved past him and turned to face him. "Why didn't you tell me what was going on?"

Wilder shut and locked the door. "Sorry, it was on a need-to-know basis."

"Well, I need to know. This is Jude again, isn't it?"

"I'm afraid so."

"That jerk!" Chester spat. "How dare he mess with Stella and now with that sweet young couple. I tell ya, I have been praying tough prayers, wanting God to smite Jude with some mighty smiting."

Wilder chuckled. "I'm with you on that one."

"So, what can I do? How can I help? I still have contacts back on the military base, and I'm not opposed to calling in some favors. And I've already contacted the CBPT."

Wilder tried to figure out which agency Chester was talking about. "CBPT?"

"Crawdad Beach Prayer Team," Chester said as though he should have known. "They are the finest group of people you'll ever meet. I asked them to pray protection prayers for Stella, Marcus, Olivia, and our town. I did not give them details, and they won't ask. They pray, knowing God knows the details and what is best for all concerned. You know, prayer is like using a smart bomb. Goes right to the heart of the matter."

"That's an interesting way to look at it." Wilder motioned

toward his pseudo-office. "Sit down, and I'll tell you what we know." Since Chester's military level still had a top-secret security clearance, he would be a definite ally in their battle against Jude. Wilder filled him in on everything he knew and what he had learned from Stella, Mia, and Robert.

Chester sat back in his chair and shook his head. "I did not see that coming. But now, it makes sense. Jude would never have escaped capture and stayed off the radar without help. I'll make a discreet phone call to a friend higher up the chain of command and see if we can't get pressure from the top down."

"Are you sure you can trust them?"

"I have no doubt they will do the right thing." Chester stood and looked his way. "Are you sure about your findings?"

Wilder blew out a breath. "Ninety-nine percent sure."

"Makes me want to curse, but instead, I'll pray." Chester shook his head and walked out the door.

Wilder contacted his team and checked everyone's status. So far, all was quiet. The bakery building and Stella's property were secure for the night.

Wilder sent a text to Mia to make sure they were doing okay. No response. Maybe she had stepped away from her phone for a moment. He dialed her number, and the call went to voice mail.

Strange. Wilder texted Stella. Again, no response. He called her cell and got her voicemail. Something wasn't right.

His pulse pounding, Wilder called the team outside Stella's house. "Get in there, now!"

Chapter 12

Head spinning, Stella forced her eyes open and tried to focus in the dingy light. Where was she? Her arms numb, she tried to move, but her wrists were handcuffed against her back, and her legs were bound. Every movement of her legs added pressure on her wrists, revealing they had hog-tied her. Her heart hammered as she struggled on the cement floor to get free.

"The lady finally awakes." The familiar voice came from a dark corner. *Jude.*

"You won't get away with this." Stella glared at her captor as he moved closer.

"That is such a cliché statement." Jude waved a dismissive hand. Getting on his knees next to her, he leaned toward her face, so close she could smell his foul breath. His dark eyes bored into hers. "Can you explain how I got inside your little house? *No*. Can you explain why no one watching the house noticed? *No.* Did anyone come to your rescue as you were carried away? *No*. So, *why* would you think I won't get away with *anything* I do to you?"

Stella shuddered at his evil smile and swallowed against the bile rising in her throat. Bible verses about not being afraid peppered her brain but were scattered and barely cohesive. Stella glanced around the room. It was empty but for her and Jude. "Where is Mia?" She hated the quivering in her voice.

"I would assume she's still at your house."

Stella tried to remember. Mia had fought with her as the masked men rushed into the office. How did they get in? And why didn't they hear the alarm or see anything on the video feeds? Blinking back the moisture in her eyes, Stella tried to be brave. "Is she okay?"

"Okay?" Jude shrugged.

Stella's breath caught in her throat as heat enveloped her body. What if her friend was dead?

Annoyance flashed over Jude's face. "Alive or dead, why would we want Mia with us?"

Was he talking about the two of them or the others who were involved? "Us?"

Jude smirked. "You picked up on that little fact, did you? Well, no matter. I'm tired of the game and tired of you. I've made you pay for your attempt to turn me in to the authorities, but there is one final payment to be made. I'll keep you for a little longer, make your friends sweat and wonder what happened to you." He put his hands around her neck and squeezed. "And then, I'll leave your body somewhere they can find it so that for the rest of their measly little lives, they will know they failed to protect you." With that statement, he released his grip on her throat, got on his feet, and left her gasping for air on the dirty floor.

Wilder's heart momentarily stopped. Stella's office looked like a tornado had ripped through, and the floor was smeared with blood. He ran to Mia. "What happened? Where's Stella?"

Mia pushed back at his people who were trying to help stop the bleeding in her leg. "They took her."

"Took her? Who took her?" He glared at his team. "How did they get into this house!"

His men averted their gaze as they mumbled excuses. Camera feeds had been hacked and looped to make it look like Stella was still sitting at her desk. Even now the screen showed her sitting there. The team in the front of the house hadn't seen anything. The man Wilder had posted at the back of Stella's house was missing. It was unclear if he had been part of her abduction, taken, or was lying somewhere dead.

Wilder clenched his fists and turned his attention back to Mia. "Tell me everything that happened."

Although Mia had been shot, thankfully, no major arteries had been hit, nor had any of her bones been damaged. She was lucky. No, she was blessed. Mia and Stella had tried to fight off three armed masked men, but Mia had been shot and received a concussion from a blow to the head. The last thing she remembered was Stella being held down and given an injection by one of the men.

Rage pulsing through his veins, Wilder drove to his main office. Rain pounded on his windshield. Thankful that Mia would be okay, he prayed whatever injection the attackers had given Stella wasn't lethal and she'd be found alive.

He should have insisted on staying with Stella. Wilder hit his steering wheel as frustration and worry pooled acid in his stomach. He threw up desperate prayers for her protection and wisdom on her location. What if Stella was already dead, or what if Jude had tortured her? Groaning, Wilder shook his head. He didn't need to let his thoughts go in that direction.

Stella had always been the nicest woman he'd ever known. Why did bad things happen to good people? In his line of work, he'd seen that fact plenty of times, which kept him from becoming a Christian for most of his life. Bad people did bad things; even people he thought were good had done bad things, but now he knew God was always good and always loving. No matter what, Wilder needed to trust that God knew everything, and no matter how someone tried to hide their evil deeds, they would not escape God's righteous judgment.

Benjamin had told him that instead of asking God why He allowed so many bad things to happen, he should ask God to help him make a difference. Wilder had done that over the last two years but wanted to do so much more.

He arrived at his facility, passed through the electronic gate, and ran to his office. God knew what was happening, but Wilder needed answers, and he needed them now!

Chapter 13

Even though I walk through the valley of the shadow of death, I will fear no evil, for You are with me; Your rod and Your staff comfort me. Stella repeated the verse in her mind over and over as she looked for a way to escape.

Gray paint covered the tiny window near the ceiling, masking the time of day. How long had she been here? Her body screamed in the pain of being bound, but no matter how she tried to move, she couldn't get free. Her bladder complained, and she desperately needed relief. How long before Jude returned? If someone didn't come soon, she would have to lie in her own filth.

Stella thought of Paul and Silas, the true-life account of being beaten and thrown in prison, and still, the men had praised God. Even David, when he was hiding in the wilderness and running from King Saul, David wrote Psalms praising God. How did they do that?

She wasn't afraid of dying; she would go to heaven since she believed Jesus Christ was her Savior. Her fear came from what might happen to her friends. What if Mia was dead and Wilder and others lost their lives because of her?

Verses from Isaiah came to mind: *fear not, for I am with you. Do not be dismayed, for I am your God; I will strengthen you. I will help you. I will uphold you with my righteous right hand. When you pass through the waters, I will be with you, and through the rivers, they will not overflow you. When you walk through the fire, you will not be scorched, nor will the flame burn you, for I am the Lord your God, the Holy One of Israel, your Savior.*

Even though God was with her, if God was telling her not to fear, did that mean He knew she would sometimes be afraid? No matter how much training she had in her profession and the number of missions she had been on, a level of fear remained.

Perfect love casts out fear. The verse washed over her, causing her to take a deep breath. God was, and is, the only perfect love, and He was with her. Another verse from Romans came, reminding her that neither death, nor life, nor angels, nor principalities, nor things present, nor things to come, nor powers, nor height, nor depth, nor any other created thing, would be able to separate her from the love of God, which is in Christ Jesus her Lord.

She breathed deep and tried to refocus. She needed to trust God. No matter what might happen.

"I don't care how many times you've gone over it. I want you to go over it again!" Wilder disconnected the call. He should have been in his main office so he could have used the landline and slammed down the phone receiver. Hanging up on a cell phone did not give the same satisfaction. Maybe he was being too hard on his team. And he probably needed to eat and get some sleep, but how could he when Stella was alone out there somewhere?

He'd had prayed and prayed some more. God knew where Stella was. Why didn't He share that fact with them? Wilder tried to quiet his thoughts and think rationally or irrationally when it came to Jude.

They had traced Jude arriving at a nearby airport, meaning he was probably still in the area. Where would he be? Wilder clicked on links using his laptop to locate rental property near Crawdad Beach. He needed to find something remote, maybe with a barn, outbuildings, or a basement.

Using the map function from the realty site, Wilder started at Crawdad Beach. Not much was available close to the city. With the sandy soil, there were hardly any basement properties. Zooming out on the map, he made note of five properties that were remote enough to be a possibility. After printing out the listings and the addresses, he checked to see which ones had been recently rented or stood vacant for over six months.

Wilder sent the information to those on his team with directions for them to check out each property. He'd take the most recent rental listing and see if Chester wanted to join him for a road trip.

"I could have been more help before now," Chester grumbled as he sat in the passenger seat of Wilder's car. "You should have called me sooner."

"You're retired. I didn't want to bother you."

"Retired? You think that's what I am?" Chester glared at him. "I'm busier than ever living in this town. You just wouldn't believe all that has happened in the last few years. We've had people in witness protection, arrested attackers, found hidden treasure, stopped cyber-attacks, you name it; Crawdad Beach has handled it."

Wilder bit back a grin. "I'm sorry. I didn't mean to criticize you or the town."

"Well, good. Let's be clear: if you are going to stay and be a Crawdadian, you need to respect other Crawdadians."

Wilder had to hold on to the steering wheel to keep from saluting. "Yes, sir."

"That's better," Chester huffed. "Now, tell me why we are heading to this property and what makes you think Stella might be there."

"It's remote and was recently rented by what looks like a shell corporation."

"Ah, you have your thinking cap on. If you think Jude is there, do you have a backup if we have any trouble?"

"My team knows where we are going. I'll message them if we see something that needs their attention."

"Fair enough. Plus, I bought Betsy with me."

"Betsy?" Wilder glanced at his friend.

Chester patted the bulge under his vest. "Yep, forty-five caliber beauty. We've been together longer than Maybelline and I have. Yes, sir, Betsy and I have been through many battles."

"Battles? Care to share?"

"Nope, sorry. Some things are between a man and his gun. Betsy never killed anyone, but she scared quite a few men and winged several others."

Wilder shook his head. The situation remained serious, but his friend lightened the mood. His turn ahead, he slowed the car.

Chester motioned with his hand. "Keep going and take the next road."

"Why? The GPS shows the property is down here."

"Trust me. I know the area around Crawdad Beach like the back of my hand. Of course, now that I'm getting older, my hands look slightly different. But, anyway, I figure we might want to come up quiet from the back of the property."

Wilder nodded. "Okay, if you're sure."

"Sure, I'm sure, or I wouldn't have said it. The property in question backs up to a wildlife management area where we've got Blackjack Oak, which is part of the Beech family, Swamp Spanish Oak, Post Oak, Red Maple, Sassafrass, Sweet Gum, Sycamore, Cabbage Palmetto, and Loblolly Pine--lots of beautiful trees. In case you were wondering, I spent a few months being a trail guide."

"Good to know." Turning the car down a quiet country road, Wilder pulled to the side and stopped the vehicle.

After they checked their weapons, they each took extra handcuffs and supplies they might need. Looking like the commanding officer Chester had once been, he hopped out and followed Wilder.

Watching and listening, they crept through the woods. Wilder stopped behind a tree and held up his hand, a stop sign in the flesh. Chester crept next to him.

Weapons in hand, a young man with a military-cut haircut stood erect on the front porch of an old farmhouse, and behind the house stood two military-looking men guarding a concrete outbuilding.

Chapter 14

Stella thanked God that Jude had let her use the bathroom. She'd barely been able to stand, much less walk the way they had kept her tied. Her hands and legs now free, Stella rubbed her sore wrists and then her bruised ankles.

While in the bathroom, Stella had heard a female voice that sounded vaguely familiar. Did it belong to someone she had met in Crawdad Beach or from her military service? Stella placed her back against the concrete wall in the corner where she could watch the door. Quieting her thoughts, she tried to place the voice she had heard. The common denominator had to be Jude which narrowed down the suspects.

Stella mentally checked off the women she'd encountered over the years. One face popped into her memory, and anger jolted through her. *Lorraine Moreno.*

Years ago, Lorraine had insisted Jude be part of the team where Stella had found him stealing government secrets. Even though Lorraine had been married at the time, it had been obvious she found Jude attractive. Had Lorraine been involved in Jude's crimes? Is that why Jude was able to escape capture? She was still high up in the chain of command and had the power to protect him. Was Lorraine still working for the government and also involved in espionage?

The thought made Stella even angrier. Getting to her feet, Stella pressed her ear against the door. Muffled voices came from down the hall. They were getting closer. She hurried to take her place back in the corner.

The door opened. Jude, gun in hand, walked toward her. "I have a surprise for you. Someone wants to see you."

Stella rose to her feet and punched his chest. "Lorraine Moreno."

Surprise crossed his face before he quickly regained composure. Jude's dark eyes narrowed to slits. "Well, aren't you the smart one?" He slapped her across the face, then grabbed her arm and pulled her out of the room and down the hall.

They couldn't wait until dark or for his team to arrive. Using hand motions, Wilder let Chester know he would take the men guarding the concrete building. His friend nodded and crept through the trees to get closer to the house.

Wilder plotted the best way to approach the building. The property had not been maintained, but beyond the tree line, the tall grass and underbrush would do nothing to hide his approach.

A muscular red-haired man leaned against the door frame; the other, a black-haired man with a bruised face, paced back and forth as though frustrated to be on guard duty. Both men carried AK-47s. Wilder couldn't help wondering if

Mia had left her mark on the one man. Bits and pieces of the men's conversation were partially audible. Both were upset with how they had been treated by Jude and had thought they would do more than merely kidnap a woman. Wilder had no doubt they would shoot if they saw him.

He glanced over to check Chester's progress, and his stomach dropped. Chester, his hair a mess, limped toward the man in front of the house. "Excuse me, but I need a phone," Chester said in a feeble voice. "The car is on another road, and I've been trying to find someone to call for help."

With gun raised, the younger man stepped off the porch. "You need to move on, gramps. We don't have a phone you can use."

"You don't?" Chester scratched his chin as though flabbergasted. "Not even a landline?" He limped closer. "I have a landline at home. My kids and grandkids want me to get one of those portable phones, but why would I want one of those?"

The young man blew out a breath and walked to where Chester stood. "I said you need to move on."

Chester looked at him like he couldn't believe anyone would talk to him like that. And then, in what seemed to be one fluid motion, Chester grabbed the man's gun, flipped the man in the dirt, and put the gun in his face. "Don't make even one little peep."

Wilder couldn't help but grin as he watched Chester cuff the man's hands behind his back and stuff a handkerchief in his mouth. Chester pushed him inside the house. If anyone were inside, he'd take care of them.

At least Wilder didn't have to worry about that situation. He glanced back at the men at the building. They were still talking and oblivious to what happened at the farmhouse. After watching how Chester had diffused the situation with the other man, Wilder checked his surroundings to rethink how best to approach the men. He almost chuckled at the thought of using a technique from his childhood.

Stooping low, Wilder moved to a clump of brush where he could watch and not be seen. Taking a branch, he rustled the leaves and let out a low grunt, then a snort.

The men stopped talking, and the black-haired one who had been pacing gazed in his direction. "Did that sound like a wild boar?"

Wilder rustled and snorted again.

Black-hair held up his weapon. "Those things will tear you up."

"Don't shoot." Red-hair grabbed the man's gun. "Jude will tear *you* up if you bring attention to where we are."

Wilder rustled the bush again and deepened his grunt to almost growl proportions.

"We can't just sit here and wait for it to attack." Black-hair set down his gun and pulled an M-9 bayonet special forces knife.

Wilder snorted. The way Black-hair conducted himself, he was not special forces. And if it had been a wild boar, a knife would only have made the animal angrier.

Knife raised, Black-hair crept closer. Wilder readied

himself and mentally counted the steps before the man would see him. Five. Four. Three. Two. One.

With a massive growl, Wilder grabbed the man's legs, knocking him to the ground and dragging him behind the brush. With a few well-placed blows, Wilder rendered the man unconscious.

Wild-eyed, Red-hair came running toward where his friend had disappeared. He stopped at the edge of the bushes and called the man's name.

Wilder rustled the bushes and hoped his deep-throated growl made the man's hair stand on end.

Chapter 15

"If you're working with Jude, you've also been selling government secrets. Why would you do that?" Rubbing her cheek where Jude had hit her, Stella glared at Lorraine. The woman was now in her sixties, yet out of uniform, she dressed like a twenty-year-old. The look was not attractive.

"That's a stupid question. Money and love are powerful forces." Lorraine put her arm around Jude and smirked at Stella like she had won a top-dollar prize.

Thinking Jude was a prize was a nauseating thought. Stella swallowed hard to keep down the bile rising in her throat.

"You were always the goody-two-shoes of the group," Lorraine continued. "Always playing by the rules, faithful to your God, country, and husband. And what has it gotten you? Nothing. You no longer work for the government, your husband is dead, and to top it off, you're living in a two-bit town."

"I have no regrets." Stella stood taller. "What do you have?"

"She has me," Jude said with a cocky swagger. "What else would a woman want?"

Stella burst out laughing. She couldn't help it. The whole

situation was ridiculous. Lorraine and Jude had spent years making other people's lives miserable, and all they had were one another.

Lorraine's eyes flared, and she grabbed Stella by the hair and yanked. Her beet-red face only inches from Stella's; she screamed obscenities.

Chuckling, Jude kissed Lorraine. "I'll take care of Stella." He grabbed Stella's arm and squeezed so forcefully that she fell to her knees. "Kneel in front of me and beg for your life."

Stella struggled back to her feet. "Never. I will never kneel before you, nor will I beg. I know where I'm going when I leave this world." Before she could duck, stars filled her vision.

She fell face-first into blackness.

Wilder cuffed and secured the men, then rushed toward the building.

Chester joined him. "I found your team member taken from Stella's. He's alive, but they worked him over pretty good. Thankfully, no broken bones. He's watching the guard. No one else is in the house."

Wilder motioned toward the door. "I heard someone screaming."

"Take a deep breath." Chester grabbed his arm. "Let's make sure we know what we might face."

Wilder did as his friend suggested. He needed to focus.

Thankfully, the door was unlocked. Opening it a few inches, he could see down an empty hall. Closed doors were on either side. He looked back at Chester and nodded.

Weapons drawn, they quietly made their way inside. The sound of raised voices came from farther down the hallway. Wilder led the way.

They checked rooms as they moved forward, then stopped outside the door, where they heard the voices. Wilder leaned closer to listen. Jude and a female voice that sounded like Lorraine Moreno were arguing. He had to temper his anger and focus. Was Stella inside? If they rushed in, would they shoot her?

Chester whispered he would go back out and use the AK-47s to send off a few bursts to get them to go outside.

Wilder nodded and kept his voice low. "Before you do that, I'll wait inside. Handle whoever comes out, and I'll look for Stella." Ducking inside one of the rooms, Wilder waited and prayed.

Gunfire blasted and echoed down the hall.

A door burst open, and Jude ran outside.

Wilder silently moved to the now open room.

His heart stopped. Was he too late?

Lorraine stood over Stella's crumpled body.

Rushing forward, he knocked the handgun out of Lorraine's hand. His anger surging like hot lava, he shoved her against the wall. It took all his strength not to break her in two.

"Wilder?" A hand touched his shoulder. He turned at the

sweet sound of Stella's voice. She was alive! He searched her bruised face. "Are you okay?" After he cuffed Lorraine and shoved her in the corner, he took Stella in his arms and held her close against his chest. "I was scared they had killed you."

"I'm very much alive and very glad to see you." She squirmed from his embrace and pointed to where Lorraine was trying to escape. "We better grab her before she gets away."

Wilder shrugged and grinned. "Chester is outside. He'll take care of Lorraine." Without another thought, Wilder took Stella back in his arms and kissed her like he had always wanted to kiss her.

Chapter 16

Early morning sunshine filtered through the trees as birds chirped and sang at the top of their little lungs. Looking out at the backyard, Stella sipped coffee as she stood at the kitchen sink. She'd slept better than she had in years and even felt young again.

Mia hobbled into the room. "How does it feel?"

Stella smiled at her friend. "It feels great. Jude and Lorraine are finally in custody, and hopefully, they will be in custody for the rest of their lives. I'm free. Finally free."

"I'm happy for you. It's about time." Mia took the coffee pot and filled her mug. "But, I was referring to something else."

"Something else?"

"Wilder's kiss."

Stella's cheeks blasted with heat as she tried to avoid her friend's mischievous grin. "It was nice."

"Nice?" Mia laughed. "You two were lip-locking and hugging for probably thirty minutes. Everyone on the team saw you together."

"They did?" How had she not noticed? Another wave of heat enveloped Stella. Had they kissed and hugged that long? Maybe that's why her lips had looked a little puffy when she got home last night. All she recalled was the feeling of Wilder's strong arms around her. Stella gave a nervous glance at her friend. "You're kidding, right?"

Mia shook her head and chuckled. "No, I'm not. I bet you don't even remember me there."

"You were there?" Stella cringed. That tipped the embarrassment scale since she had no recollection of anyone other than Wilder.

"Yep. And, I must say, seeing you two engaged in mutual affection was long overdue. You belong together. Benjamin would approve. The week before he passed, he had a feeling something was going to happen to him."

Stella held onto the kitchen counter. "But Benjamin never said anything to me." She tried to think back to the week before he passed. They had visited the bank and checked their online accounts to ensure they were in order, but they had done that every few years to keep all their accounts up to date. Had Benjamin tried to tell her, and she didn't listen? No. She couldn't remember anything other than he had told her he loved her more than usual. Stella looked at Mia. "Why would he tell you?" The thought Benjamin told Mia and not her stung.

"I'm your best friend, remember?" Mia touched Stella's arm. "Don't be hurt. He said he was planning on talking to you, but well, I guess he never got that chance. But back to Wilder. He's a good guy. It's time to be open to love again."

"Love? That isn't even on my radar." Stella looked away. That wasn't exactly true. The thought of loving again hadn't entered her mind until recently, until Wilder came back into her life. She shook her head and turned back to Mia. "Being in Wilder's arms was nice, but we haven't discussed a relationship. I'm not ready. The thought of marrying again is terrifying. I'm not a spring chicken anymore."

"You may be an autumn chicken, but you are still a beautiful woman."

Stella held up her hand. "Let's not talk about this. Okay? I just want to get on with my life and enjoy not worrying about Jude or anything else." Stella finished her coffee, grabbed her purse, and put five dollars in her pocket. She needed to get outside, walk, and do something to calm down.

Sidestepping her friend, Stella turned off the alarm and stepped out of the house. Why hadn't Benjamin told her first that he felt something would happen to him? Had what Mia said the other day about Stella's pride and trust issues kept everyone at arm's length, including Benjamin?

Stella stomped down the Main Street sidewalk and kept walking until she reached the park. She didn't even slow her step to admire the Crepe myrtles in full bloom and colorful flowers. Instead, she followed the trail that meandered next to the riverbank.

Why did Mia mention love? Stella had her chance with Benjamin. She didn't need another man in her life. No siree. She would be just fine, just God and her together again—just like old times.

She had been blessed with a wonderful, kind, attentive husband. How could she ever love or trust another man?

Wilder's face kept popping into her thoughts. She swatted at the air, wishing she could swipe away the memory of Wilder's handsome face and sweet hugs and kisses.

Stella growled. Her thoughts were a jumbled mess. She needed to calm down and focus. Stopping at a bench, she sat beside the lazy river. She'd prayed for decades for help and relief from Jude's attacks, and her rescue hadn't come as soon as she had hoped, but God *had* rescued her.

Sounds in the tree branch above her drew Stella's attention. A momma squirrel with two babies watched her as their tails twitched. Stella sighed.

God had watched over her and was still watching over her. Throughout her life, God was faithful. Had she been as loyal to God? She needed to let go of the past, trust God, and step into whatever future He had planned.

Wilder stood at his desk in the main office. He had kissed women before but never experienced kisses like with Stella. What was the difference? He scratched his chin. Maybe because he had taken himself off the dating market once he became a Christian, he had forgotten what kissing was like. He scoffed a chuckle. No, that wasn't it. Kissing Stella had felt pure.

Why would he think that? Maybe it was because he didn't have ulterior motives when he kissed her; he just wanted her to know he was there for her, loved her, and wanted to cherish her.

He stacked the boxes he had filled with his personal belongings and took one final look around his office. Now that Stella was safe, he'd finally retired. He'd stay in touch in an advisory role, but the paperwork had been finalized and signed for the sale of his company, and his Vice President would step in as the new president. The team waited in the break room to give Wilder a going away party.

Feeling surprisingly content, happy, and fulfilled, Wilder picked up his boxes to take to his car. He always thought he'd be killed on a mission or continue working as long as possible, yet here he was, heading into retirement.

He still wasn't exactly sure what he would do once he stepped away from the company he founded. At least he had a substantial nest egg to start a new life. And that life, he hoped and prayed, would be with one beautiful, green-eyed woman.

Chapter 17

Tantalizing smells of fresh-baked pastries made Stella's mouth water. She pointed to the cinnamon rolls in the bakery display case. "Could I have that one, please?"

"Of course." Olivia placed the pastry on a small plate and handed it to Stella. "This one is on the house. Marcus and I are grateful you are okay."

"Thank you. I'm grateful Jude and the others are now in custody."

"We are, too." Olivia's brown eyes misted. "Marcus's dad told us how long everything had been going on. I'm so sorry you had to live that way."

"God helped me through." Stella wasn't just saying that; she meant every word. Without God's help, she would have never lived this long.

"Would you like a cup of coffee?"

"No, thank you. I had some earlier this morning." Stella took her pastry and found a table by the window. On the sidewalk outside, Marcus's sister Alexa, who had a lightning bolt shaved in her hair, zipped past. An older couple walked a little white dog. Stella grinned. It was so nice to people watch without worry.

Every day, the little town felt more like home. *Home.* Her

home used to be with Benjamin, but when he was gone their house had only been where they had lived.

Stella nibbled on her roll. Mia had been a good friend for decades, and they would always stay friends, but now that Jude had been caught, it was only a matter of time before she left. Would Wilder also leave town? Stella stared out the window. She'd be alone again since she didn't have children or family. God promised never to leave or forsake His children, but that didn't mean they wouldn't at times feel lonely.

"May I join you?" With a cup of coffee in hand, Henry Doss stood next to her table. He looked a few years older than her, and his kind, welcoming eyes made her feel comfortable like he was an older brother. She'd always wanted a sibling.

"Yes, please."

He sat across from her. "I heard the good news. We have been praying for you, and now we are praying you can relax and enjoy being here."

"Thank you. I appreciate your prayers more than you know.

Henry smiled. "I'd like to invite you to church this weekend. After the service, my family, along with Chester and Maybelline, will be gathering for lunch at my grandson's house, and we would love to have you join us. Please don't worry about bringing anything. We always have plenty to share."

Stella had planned on visiting the church. "That's very sweet of you. Thank you."

"Great." His blue eyes sparkled. "Meet me in the lobby after the service, and you can ride with one of us, or we will give you directions." Henry gave her his phone number and stood. "Don't hesitate to call if you have questions."

Taking a bite of the melt-in-your-mouth cinnamon roll, Stella smiled. Maybe she wouldn't be lonely after all.

Wilder set the boxes of his belongings in his apartment and took a water bottle from his refrigerator. Home sweet temporary home. He opened the French doors leading into a screened-in covered patio and sat in one of the chairs. Vibrant flowers bordered the manicured lawn. Chester and Maybelline lived in the house behind the duplex, and their yard was also beautifully maintained.

Taking a swig of his water, Wilder leaned back. Would Crawdad Beach be somewhere he would want to live long-term? As nice as the little town was, he probably wouldn't stay if Stella saw him only as a friend. Then again, would he be man enough just to be her friend?

There were too many questions without answers. Wilder would stay, pray, and see what was next. His phone signaled an incoming message. The text made his blood boil. Jude admitted to killing Benjamin. Jude had paid someone to slip drugs into Benjamin's coffee when he went to his favorite coffee shop before work. Stella had been correct that her husband didn't die of natural causes.

Anger surging through Wilder, he clenched his fists. Benjamin had been his best friend. Even before knowing Jude had killed Benjamin, it probably was a good thing he had been with Stella when Jude was taken into custody.

He needed to tell Stella about Benjamin's death. Wilder couldn't imagine her reaction, but he would be there for whatever she needed.

Fifteen minutes later, Wilder stood at Stella's front door waiting. Where was she, and where was Mia? He stepped back and stared at the security camera. Was Stella avoiding him? Maybe he shouldn't have kissed her. Had he screwed up his chances with her before he even had a chance with her?

Wilder blew out a breath and walked toward his car. He stopped when he noticed Stella walking down the street toward him.

"Good morning!" She called as she came closer.

"Good morning." He tried to read her expression. Stella seemed pleased to see him. At least he hoped she was glad he was there. She didn't even seem nervous. Maybe their shared hugs and kisses didn't affect her like it did him.

Stella held up her phone. "I saw you on the security camera. I would have said something, but I was almost home." Using her cell, she turned off her alarm, opened the door, and turned toward him. "Would you like to come in?"

"Yeah, thanks." Wilder followed her inside and waited until she sat in a chair. He settled on the couch across from her.

"What brings you out on this fine morning?"

Wilder rubbed his palms on his jeans. "I have some difficult information to share with you?"

"Oh." Stella sat straighter. "Please tell me Jude and Lorraine didn't escape."

"No, they are behind bars for the rest of their lives."

Her shoulders relaxed. "Good."

"I'm afraid it's about something Jude shared with the authorities."

Stella's lips thinned. "He killed Benjamin, didn't he?"

Wilder felt his eyebrows raise. "Yes. I'm so sorry."

She rose from her chair and went to stand by the front window. "I knew it. I knew Jude was behind what happened to Benjamin." Her face still calm, she glanced toward Wilder. "Did Jude say how he did it?"

Wilder came next to her. "Yes, he paid someone to slip drugs into Benjamin's coffee at the coffee shop."

Her hands clasped in front of her, Stella stood still, her gaze focused out the window. Her bottom lip had the slightest tremble, and moisture built in her eyes.

Taking a chance that it would be okay, Wilder pulled her into an embrace. "I'm sorry, Stella." At first, her body was stiff in his arms, then relaxed, and her arms came around him as she laid her head on his chest and cried.

Chapter 18

Wiping her tears, Stella stepped away from Wilder. "I'm sorry. I shouldn't have."

Wilder's eyebrows raised. "Shouldn't have cried? Shouldn't have let me hug you? You just found out your husband had been murdered; it's okay to be upset." He reached toward her.

Stella shook her head as she backed away. "No, I'm fine." She sat in her chair, folded her hands in her lap, and tried to compose herself. "Thank you for telling me. I'm grateful Jude will be punished for his many crimes."

Confusion evident on Wilder's face; he just stood there looking at her. "Okay. I guess I'll be going."

She sucked in a breath. "Please don't go." She didn't want to be alone; no, it was more than that; she wanted Wilder near her. Why did she keep fighting her emotions and fighting him? He obviously cared for her.

Wilder's gaze never left her face as he rubbed his hand along his chin and settled on the couch.

"I'm sorry. I'm not good at this." She waved her hand back and forth between them.

"This?" Leaning forward, he rested his elbows on his knees. "I care for you, Stella. I always have and always will."

His deep voice washed over her.

"Why?" She didn't mean to say the thought out loud. How could he care for her?

Wilder's smile was gentle. "When I first met you, I wanted you." He held up his hand. "Not in a bad way. I wanted what you had. My attraction for you wasn't just that you're beautiful, kind, and sweet; I wanted to know who lived in you. You always had a peace that I couldn't get. You and Benjamin tried to tell me it was Jesus Christ, but I fought for so long. God's grace finally got a hold of me, and I've waited to give you time to grieve over Benjamin. He was a great guy, and I can't take his place. But I want to spend time with you, whether as a friend or more than a friend. Either way, I'm here for you as long as you will have me."

Tears stung as she tried to swallow the lump in her throat. Could it be true that Wilder cared for her? Wilder had been their friend for decades. Could she take the chance on a relationship? The thought was terrifying. What did she have to offer someone like him?

Would stepping over the friendship barrier be strange? The fact that she was sitting here thinking about it meant it *was* strange. She needed to get back to the safety of her computer world, where she could write code to do her bidding. Wilder was a wild card with too many variables. But he was so sweet. Could she take a chance and step out into the unknown dating world? She shuddered. Dating at her age? Ack!

Grinning, Wilder came and bent down to catch her

attention. "It doesn't have to be difficult, you know. We're friends. We can take this," He waved his hand back and forth between them, "one day at a time."

Her lip trembling, Stella looked into his handsome face. "I am scared to death."

"I promise to treat your heart very gently." Wilder pulled her up from her chair and embraced her. "Let's see where our friendship leads."

In his strong arms, Stella took a deep breath. Maybe she could do this, take a leap, and see what might happen next.

Wilder stopped his car and parked in the church lot. After he had left Stella the previous day, he still had questions about where they stood. He'd thought she was open to moving forward in the relationship, but now he wasn't sure. He'd prayed and had some semblance of peace about them. Maybe at church, he'd get some answers.

As Wilder stepped into the church lobby, he spotted Chester.

His friend hurried toward him and gave him a side-arm bro hug. "Good to see you, Wilder." Chester motioned toward a white-haired gentleman with blue eyes. "Let me introduce you to my friend, Henry Doss."

The man with the most piercing, friendly blue eyes smiled and shook Wilder's hand. "Welcome. We're glad you're here."

"Thank you."

"Wilder Templeton." Maybelline smiled as she walked toward him and enveloped him in a big hug. "It is good to see you. I'm so glad you're here."

He chuckled with relief. "I'm grateful you're glad." The last time he had seen Maybelline, she was not happy with him, not one bit since he had been a real jerk before he became a Christian.

"No worries. All is forgiven. You must sit with us." She grabbed her arm and led him to a pew about midway down the auditorium.

Wilder grinned when he saw who was already sitting there.

Stella glanced up, did a double-take, and smiled.

Wilder slid into the pew next to her. "I didn't know you would be here."

"I didn't know you would be either, but I am delighted you're here."

At Stella's sweet smile, Wilder sat a little taller. Maybe she was open to going beyond a simple friendship after all.

Chapter 19

The sermon was wonderful, and seeing people Stella already knew from town made the time even sweeter, especially since she sat next to Wilder. During worship, he sang in a deep baritone perfect-pitch voice. When she took a quick peek at his Bible, it showed highlights and notes indicating he studied God's word. The changes since he became a Christian were incredibly amazing and very attractive.

After the service ended, they both were invited to Henry's grandson's house for lunch. The experience had been a fun, although overwhelming, experience since Henry's family included Henry's dog, Filbert, his daughter, Katherine, her husband, Michael, and their two children, Tess with her husband Paul, and their twins, and David and his wife Marie, and their twins, along with their little dog, Filbertina. Henry's other daughter, Crystal, and her husband, Eric, were there, along with Crystal's daughter, Olivia, and her husband, Marcus. Henry's sister, Helen, was with her great-nephew, Jeremy, and his wife, Grace. Even Chester and Maybelline were there as though they had been part of the family forever.

Stella grinned that she could remember each person's name and relation to one another. She couldn't imagine having a big family like that. Even Wilder had fit in talking, visiting with the adults, and playing with the children and dogs.

"You seemed to enjoy yourself," Wilder said as he walked her to her car.

"I did." Stella opened her car door and turned toward him. "I can't believe how welcoming they made us feel. It was nice and not awkward at all. Do you remember everyone's names?"

Wilder shook his head. "Not sure about that, but I can give you a description of each one."

Stella chuckled. "With your background, you can probably give their weight and height."

A dimple showed with his grin. "Probably. I did find it interesting how much Henry's family kept studying your eyes. Since Henry's mom had green eyes like yours, they wondered if there was a connection. I thought they were about to take your blood sample and send it off for a DNA test since your eyes are a gorgeous and unusual shade of green. Is that color that uncommon?"

"A DNA test would have been interesting, but I doubt I have any living relatives. I did research eye color once and found that only two percent of people have green eyes."

"I knew you were one in a billion." Wilder wiggled his eyebrows.

She did so enjoy being with him and wasn't ready for their time together to end. "Want to come over to my place?"

Wilder tapped his chin and seemed to contemplate her question, then leaned closer. "Thank you for the invite, but how about I give you time to change and then drive you to the beach? I'm not much into swimming but am a good beach walker."

With the sunny day and the temperature not too hot, walking next to Wilder sounded like a great plan. "That sounds very nice."

"Great." He glanced at his watch. "Will twenty minutes give you enough time?"

"Yes. I'll be waiting." Feeling like she was sixteen and going on a date, Stella hurried home and changed into a lightweight, casual floral dress and sandals. She did a little happy dance, then stopped. She wasn't sixteen; she was a woman, an older woman.

Getting into a relationship at this time of her life was not what she thought would happen. She hadn't made contingencies to have a life with someone other than Benjamin.

Wilder was wonderful, but was she ready? And would she ever be ready?

With a beach blanket tucked under one arm, Wilder held Stella's hand as they walked along the beach. He'd imagined what it would be like to be with her, and today had far exceeded his expectations.

Ahead and to the right, a group of teenagers played beach volleyball. Sunbathers lay on the sand while a group of young men sat in chairs, ogling any female who walked by. Wilder tempered his disdain when he remembered he had done the same when he was younger.

Stella had been quiet, and he wasn't sure what she was thinking. To play it safe, he'd keep the conversation light. He squeezed her hand. "What's Mia up to these days?"

"She left a note on the kitchen table that she was out of town working on her tan and would return next week. I imagine she is somewhere in the Caribbean with her new man."

"Who is she dating these days?"

Her gaze forward, Stella increased her step. "Not sure, but this one sounds serious."

"I hope it works out okay for her."

Stella stopped and dropped his hand. "I'm sorry. This is just too weird."

"What? What did I do?"

"It's not you." She wrung her hands together. "I guess I'm just not ready. And as much as I enjoy being with you, I keep expecting Benjamin to walk up."

"That won't happen, but if it bothers you, I'll just stay beside you. Is that okay?"

Stella blew out a shuddering breath and crossed her arms over her chest. "I just didn't expect anything after Benjamin died. I thought I'd be alone. I'd be with God, but not with another man."

Wilder took a deep breath. A seagull screeched overhead, making a sound of how he was feeling. What was he supposed to do now? He thought things were progressing. Instead, he was back to square one.

Spotting a quiet place away from the ocean, he motioned for her to follow. Wilder placed the blanket on the sand and waited for her to sit. He settled beside her but not too close. Should he ask her what was going on? Or should he just stay quiet? He could handle interrogations, but women and their emotions, not so much.

Pulling her knees up, she wrapped her arms around them. "I'm sorry, Wilder. I wanted things to be different."

Not trusting that he wouldn't say the right thing, he nodded and kept his gaze on the ocean. He needed help, so he prayed for wisdom.

"I don't want to hurt you," she mumbled.

Well, that statement hurt. Here they were on a date that wasn't a date, and she was already talking about hurting him. "I am not sure what to do. How can I help?"

Stella nibbled on her lip. "I don't know."

"If it's okay, could I just process out loud?" At her nod, he continued. "This is all new. I get it. As far as I know, Benjamin was your first and only love. And here I am asking you to take a chance with me, and that's scary."

Her eyes watery, she nodded.

Wilder kept his voice gentle. "Okay, you know computers. When working on a program, you have an end goal, ideas for getting there, and what kind of code needs to be written. Thinking about being with me beyond friendship is something you have never done. You don't have the code, do you?"

"No, and that's terrifying."

"Why not look at it as an exciting adventure? Stella, I'm not out to hurt you. That would be the last thing I would ever want, but please give me a chance. Give us a chance. We can take our time, move slowly, and pray about what is best for both of us. Okay?"

Her face scrunched up like she was going to cry. "I'm sorry."

Well, he gave it his best shot. Wilder got to his feet and walked to where the waves lapped the shoreline. He'd leave Crawdad Beach and figure out what he would do next. At least he hadn't sold his house and was only renting for the next few months. The shame of it was, besides not having Stella, he liked the little town.

"Wilder?" Stella stood next to him and took his hand in hers. "I'm sorry I've made this difficult. But I really want to try because I really like you."

Squeezing her fingers, he turned toward her. "Then, we will take it one day at a time."

Her beautiful green eyes stared up at him as she bit her lip. "Could I have a hug, please?"

Wilder smiled, took her gently into his arms, and kissed the top of her head. "It's going to be okay, Stella." He held her against him and internally prayed for God's help. He also sent up a few more prayers for God's favor that she would allow them to move forward to a long-term committed relationship because whatever time he had left, he wanted it to be with the woman he'd always loved.

Chapter 20

Stella spent the morning searching for vulnerabilities in her current client's operating system, network, and databases and made notes of any potential weaknesses. She'd been in the computing industry for her entire career, and the ever-changing cyber-landscape kept her busy and satisfied. She was good at her job and enjoyed protecting others from cyber threats.

Computers she understood but was clueless about what she might face with Wilder. After their time on the beach, he had brought her home, and she'd spent much of the night praying, tossing, turning, and wondering what would happen next.

The only man she'd ever dated had been Benjamin. With his proper English background, he had been a proper gentleman before and during marriage. In contrast, Wilder had been a wild man. Yes, he had changed, but he knew things she probably never knew when it came to dating. Plus, she was older now and still inexperienced.

During difficult times, she relied on God and could quote Bible verses on being brave, not worrying, and having faith in God's help. But with Wilder, what was she supposed to do? The verse came to mind about trusting the Lord with all her heart, not leaning on her own understanding, and submitting to God in all her ways, and He'd make her paths straight. Okay, she didn't need to rely on herself. She'd trusted God with the bad in her life; it was time to trust God with the good.

Stella took a deep breath. Instead of constantly expecting something negative to happen, she needed to live in the moment and enjoy every moment given by God. Yes, she needed carpe deim ad maiorem Dei gloriam or seize the day for the greater glory of God. The thought made the hair on her arms stand at attention. Stella grinned. Even her body was ready to seize the day. Okay, maybe she could do this.

Her stomach rumbled, reminding her that she needed to eat something for lunch. The protein bar she'd had for breakfast had definitely worn off. Stella closed her projects, walked to the kitchen, and checked through the refrigerator and cabinets. The choices were way too limited.

Maybe Wilder would meet her for lunch at Tiddlywinks. But was that proper behavior in the dating world? Would he think she was forward? Oh, good grief. Didn't she just tell herself to trust God and seize the day for the greater glory of God? Stella picked up her cell phone and sent Wilder a text.

The house alarm beeped, and she checked the video footage. Mia was home? Didn't she say she would be gone until next week? Stella hurried to find her friend dragging her suitcase through the family room.

"Don't even ask. Men are such jerks." Mia entered the code on her section of the house and shut the door behind her.

Stella stood there for a moment. Should she leave her friend alone? No, she needed to make sure she was okay. Stella knocked and waited.

"Go away." Mia's muffled voice made it clear she was in no mood to talk.

A message signaled on Stella's phone. She stared at the text telling her that Wilder was heading back to town but would meet her at Tiddlywinks in fifteen minutes. Oh no. The timing was not good. Should she cancel and see if Mia might need her? Stella tapped again on the closed door. "Can I help?"

"No! Go away!"

Stella groaned. "I might go to Tiddlywinks to eat lunch. Can I bring you anything?"

"No. Leave me alone."Mia's voice broke. Oh no, she was crying. Mia didn't even cry when she had been shot.

Stella paced back and forth in the hallway. What had happened? Mia had been excited to spend time with her special man, who must have turned out to be a jerk.

Her friend needed her. Even if Stella had to sit on the floor outside Mia's door all night, she wouldn't leave.

Stella sent a text to Wilder apologizing and asking if they could do it another time.

Wilder stepped into his apartment and glanced at his phone. Stella had cancelled. Had she gotten scared again? He felt like he was living in a yo-yo world with Stella's up and down emotions. He wouldn't keep playing this game; it was time to take action. He wasn't going to let Stella get away.

Twenty minutes later, Wilder rang her doorbell and stood on the front porch with a bouquet of red roses. No matter how Stella pulled away from him, he would pursue her.

The door opened, and Stella smiled, but her eyes looked troubled. "Oh, Wilder, thank you. They are beautiful." She took the roses from him and took a deep sniff. "I'm so sorry I had to cancel." She stepped aside and motioned for him to follow. She crossed the family room and stopped in the kitchen, where she put the roses in a vase. "Mia got home early, and something happened to upset her."

"I'm sorry to hear that. Can I do anything?"

"I don't know what we can do. Mia hasn't talked to me yet. Just shut herself in her room." Stella kept her voice low. "She was crying."

"Oh, man, Mia never cries."

"I know." Stella sat at the kitchen table. "This must be serious."

He took the chair across from her. "I hate to hear about Mia, but I was worried when you texted that you were canceling because of me."

"No." Stella took a deep breath and let it out slowly. "I think I'm ready for us to date."

He chuckled at her intense expression. "Sure do look happy about this."

"No, I am happy. It's still strange. Wilder, I never dated

anyone but Benjamin."

"Oh." Now, it was making more sense—no wonder she had been worried. Benjamin had been a straight-laced, proper, well-bred, pure-blood gentleman, and Wilder was basically a wild mongrel before he met Christ. He leaned toward Stella. "I understand better now. But let me make something clear. Even though I've been a Christian for almost two years, this will be the first time I've dated since then, so it's new to me, too. I'm a new creation, and the old has passed away. Maybe, like Saul became Paul after he was saved, you could call me by my middle name, James."

Stella grinned. "James does sound tamer, but you will always be Wilder to me."

"I hope that's a good thing."

"Yes, it is. Okay, we will take it one day at a time."

"Great." His grin was probably bordering on idiotic, but he didn't care. Things were finally looking up. "Let's not overthink the dating thing. Let's just enjoy being together." Wilder reached toward her.

Smiling, she placed her hand in his and squeezed. "Okay. We are now officially dating."

Now, he just had to figure out what to do next.

Chapter 21

Her heart fluttering with excitement, Stella felt like a teenager again. She was actually going to date Wilder.

"Well, it's about time." Wearing jogging clothes, Mia entered the kitchen and leaned against the cabinet by the sink.

Feeling like she had been caught doing something she shouldn't, Stella withdrew her hand from Wilder and turned to her friend. "Are you okay?"

Mia sighed. "Yeah, this one just threw me for a loop. I thought we had a shot, but no. He was still in touch with his ex, and I do mean physically in touch."

"Ouch. I'm sorry."

Wilder growled. "I'm sorry, Mia. Can I do anything to help?"

"No, thank you, though. Stella, would you mind if I stayed here longer? I'm not sure what I'll do now."

"Of course. Stay as long as you need."

"Thanks. I'm going to go for a run and see if I can't sweat out some frustration. You two behave."

After Mia left, Wilder gazed at Stella. "I feel bad for Mia."

"Yeah, she thought he was the one." How awful to have dated and thought everything would work out. She knew Mia would bounce back, but broken hearts were harder to heal.

Wilder came around to where Stella was sitting. "It doesn't mean it will happen to us. We will pray for Mia and pray for us." Taking the hand he offered, she rose to her feet. "Since you probably haven't eaten, how about we head to Tiddlywinks for lunch?" He put his arms around her.

At the thought of eating, Stella's stomach rumbled. "I think that's a yes."

"Want me to drive?"

"How about we walk over and burn a few calories? I might need dessert from the bakery once we finish."

He kissed the top of her head. "You are truly a woman after my own heart."

After a nice walk, tempting smells met her as she entered Tiddlywinks restaurant. Wilder led her to an empty table in the back of the crowded restaurant.

Stella picked up one of the menus on the table, graced with a little cartoon crawdad wearing a chef's hat.

"What are you having?" Wilder asked.

"Grilled chicken, green beans, and corn. How about you?"

"What I had the last time. Chicken fried steak, okra, and collard greens. I love this place. Southern cooking at its finest." Wilder glanced over Stella's shoulder and stiffened.

She glanced behind her. Nothing looked out of the ordinary. People sat at their tables, talking and enjoying their meals. A dark-haired man with graying temples paid for a purchase at the take-out counter. Stella looked at Wilder. "Is something wrong?"

His gaze flitted back to her. "No, it's okay. Just thought I saw someone I recognized."

"You will probably see people you recognize every time you come to town."

He nodded. "Yeah, you're right." He smiled but still seemed on edge.

"Want to tell me what's going on?"

"No worries. I need to remember I'm retired and can just enjoy myself."

Stella grinned and raised an eyebrow. "It's a novel idea for you, isn't it?"

"Yeah, retirement wasn't on my agenda. I was going to work as long as I could. I'm officially retired, but I still plan on doing some consulting. How long do you intend to work?"

"As long as I can. I enjoy the work."

The waitress took their order, and Wilder excused himself. He walked toward the restrooms, took his phone from his back pocket, and disappeared down the hallway.

Wilder disconnected the call and took a deep breath. Xavier Gunderson was in the area. The criminal had slipped through their fingers for years. What was he doing in Crawdad Beach?

Wilder walked back to the table. The food had already been served, and Stella sat waiting for him.

"Sorry about that." He slid into his seat and placed his napkin on his lap. Since Stella continued to look at him, he wasn't sure if she was waiting for him to pick up his fork or pray. He took the safe route, bowed his head, and quietly prayed out loud.

When he finished, she smiled and started eating.

Wilder dug into his meal. At least he had passed the prayer in public test.

Stella ate for a few minutes, then laid down her fork. "I just figured out who I think that was." She leaned closer. "Xavier Gunderson."

So she had noticed him too. Wilder nodded. "Yeah, I can't believe he's here. He's been off the radar for three years."

"After we eat, let's go to my place and see what we need to do."

As soon as they stepped into her house, Stella motioned for him to follow her into her office. Her fingers flew across her computer keyboard as information and photos on Xavier filled several screens. "The last location I found for him was in Europe." She turned toward Wilder. "He must have traveled to the States using one of his assumed names. I wonder what he is up to?"

"Xavier is a career criminal and since the military base is close by, that means he's up to something, and that something isn't good. I called the base and left a message with one of my buddies. I also called my old company, and they will probably send a team to the area. We also might want to warn Mia. Didn't she have a run-in with Xavier several years ago?"

Stella nodded with a chuckle. "Oh yeah, she did. Mia is probably still angry that he was able to get away. I will let her know to watch for him." She sent a quick text to her friend.

Wilder gave Stella an apologetic look. "I'm sorry this is not how I wanted our dating to begin."

She waved a hand. "Honestly, I was somewhat concerned about what we would do on a date. We've known one another for years. It's not like we would sit around and talk to discover details about one another's life."

"True, but I'm sure there are many things about you that I don't know."

"That goes without saying. And there will always be something new to discover." Her smile made Wilder's pulse ratchet up several notches. "And, since Xavier is an unsavory character, perhaps we should ensure you are adequately prepared."

"Besides having an eighth-degree black belt and other martial arts skills, I have additional precautions." Wilder patted his leg where his holstered gun sat against his calf.

Stella's look showed admiration. "I had forgotten you were a black belt. I only made it to a red belt."

Wilder couldn't help but grin at this remarkable woman and their fun banter. "Besides your computer skills, you've also received marksmanship awards."

"Yes, but thankfully, I haven't needed to utilize that talent."

"Maybe we could visit the gun range sometime to practice."

She sent him a saucy grin. "Now, that sounds like a fun date."

Even with a known criminal in the area, Stella seemed to be enjoying herself. What happened to the hesitant, scared woman from a few days ago? He wasn't sure what caused the change, but he was in love with this woman, and there was no way anyone would mess up their lives together.

Chapter 22

The heat of embarrassment flamed up Stella's back and settled on her cheeks as she stared at Mia. "Are you sure?"

Mia chuckled as she pointed to the computer screen with Xavier's photo. "Yes, you two need to get a life. Xavier Gunderson is dead. Interpol eliminated him last week. Whoever you thought is in town is not Xavier."

Wilder gave them both a sheepish expression as he ran a hand through his hair. "At least we didn't grab the man we saw at Tiddlywinks."

Stella giggled, then laughed. "Oh, my goodness. Can you imagine?"

"I better make some apology calls." With a groan, Wilder got to his feet and left the room.

Mia laughed. "I cracked up when you sent that text about Xavier being here. Thanks for the laugh. It helped me get out of my depressing mood. So, now that you are dating Wilder, what are your plans besides watching for spies and criminals?"

"I'm not sure since I'm clueless about how to date anyone, especially Wilder."

"Well, I would give you some pointers, but I don't know if they would apply to your situation. I think you should bypass the whole dating thing and get married."

"Married?" Suddenly dizzy, Stella laid her head on her desk. "I can't think about that step if I can't even think about dating."

"Oh, good grief. You're a grown woman who has spent your career ridding the world of cyber-criminals, and you are worried about going on a date?"

"Yes, I don't know what to do." Stella whimpered.

"Just take it slow if you have to go slow. Which is very boring."

"Dating is usually about getting to know someone, and I already know Wilder."

"That's true and therefore back to my suggestion. Just get married and forego all the drama."

Stella raised her head. "Keep your voice down. Wilder might come in at any moment."

"Stop worrying, let him decide about the dating thing and enjoy being with him. Wilder should have plenty of experience."

Stella whimpered again. "That's what worries me the most."

Mia propped her backside on the desk. "Oh, now I get it. Wilder has been a man about town, and you have been isolated for most of your life. I guess that would be scary."

"What's scary?" Wilder said as he stepped into the room.

"Cobras, pythons, and alligators," Mia said without missing a beat.

Wilder sent a curious look at them. "We will try to avoid those." He sat next to Stella. "I smoothed things over with my contacts, who probably are still laughing. I guess retirement won't be as easy as I hoped."

Mia stood and patted his shoulder. "I think it's time you two unplugged from the world and did some things you've always wanted to do." Smiling, she walked to the door and closed it behind her.

Wilder's charming grin made Stella feel faint again. He was definitely a very handsome man. She nibbled on her lip. What were they supposed to do now?

Wilder tilted his head. "Since our day has been rerouted from criminal hunting, would you care to join me for a walk by the river?"

Stella blinked a few times, trying to clear her head. "That sounds nice. We could do that."

"Good." Wilder stood and pulled her to her feet as his gaze rested on her lips. Instead of kissing her, he motioned toward the door. "After you."

Wilder directed Stella to a bench facing the lazy river and waited until she settled before sitting beside her. "This doesn't have to be so difficult, you know." At her curious look, he continued. "Dating. There aren't any rules, Stella. We get to decide what we will do. What are you scared of?"

She shot him a cute grin. "Cobras, pythons, and alligators?"

He chuckled. "I will do my best to protect you from any

of those creatures. Seriously though, how can I help you relax?"

Stella placed her hands in her lap. "I'm not sure. I don't know what to expect, and that scares me."

"So, part of the problem is the unknown?" At her quick nod, Wilder plowed ahead. "Okay. Well, every day, you deal with challenges in your cyber-world, how is this different?"

Her gaze serious, Stella turned toward him. "I do not know your code."

He laughed. "Stella, I don't know yours either. We're starting from square one. I know you, but I want to know you better."

"There's not much to tell." She mumbled.

"What is making you so nervous?"

She shook her head, vehemently shook her head. "I can't tell you that."

"Now you have me very curious."

Stella stood and started walking.

He caught up with her and kept in step. "Please tell me."

She stopped and faced him. "I have never been with another man, and I know you have been with many women." Her face reddening, she looked away. "What if I don't kiss right or do other things right? What if you aren't pleased with me?"

Wilder took her in his arms. "Stella, I'm sorry. I wish my past were different. If I could change things, I would, but I can't. All I can tell you is that you are the woman I want to be with. I love you, and no one compares to you."

Chapter 23

It was a good thing Wilder was holding Stella because her legs seemed to have lost most of the ability to keep her standing. Wilder loved her? Stella took a deep breath. She knew he cared for her, but he had actually said the words. Was she supposed to say it back to him? She thought she loved him, but if she said she loved him, the words would hang out in the atmosphere. She needed to be sure.

"May I kiss you?" Wilder's deep voice made her woozy again.

Woozy? She'd never been woozy in her life. "Yes, if that's what you would like."

He swallowed his laugh. "I would hope you would *want* me to kiss you."

"Oh, I do. It's just funny you asked."

"Then I won't ask again." Wilder tilted her head up, and his lips met hers.

A moan escaped her. It wasn't the first time they had kissed, but this one scored off the Richter scale. Benjamin had been a lovely kisser, but Wilder. Wow! His kisses made her weak in the knees, which was a fascinating experience.

Wilder pulled back and gave her a look of admiration. "Stella, you are a wonderful kisser."

"Really?" The thought made her stand a little taller. "You're not just saying that?"

"No, this was the best ever." He gently ran his hand down her cheek. "I believe your lips should receive an award." He grinned. "Let's drive to the grocery store and pick up a gallon of mint chocolate chip ice cream."

Warmth flooded through her at his thoughtfulness. "You remembered that's my favorite?"

Wilder leaned his forehead against hers. "I remember many things about you. Like you said, you used to have a musical soundtrack in your head."

Stella felt her eyes go wide as she backed away. "I told you that?"

His grin sweet, he nodded. "Many years ago, you said when you were younger, you listened to music and danced when no one was watching. And that as you went about your day, the music played in your head to help you get through tough times."

She couldn't believe Wilder remembered something she had told him decades ago. Benjamin preferred symphonic tunes, so Stella went along with his choices. Maybe it was time to download and enjoy a few of her old favorites.

A few minutes later, Wilder held her hand as they entered the local grocery store, walked to the frozen food section, and pointed to the shelves of ice cream. "Do you like that brand?"

Stella nodded. "That would be perfect. Could we even buy cones and make it even more special?" She loved the crunch of a good ice cream cone.

Wilder's lips curved upward. "If that's what makes you happy, I'll be glad to oblige." He took a gallon of ice cream off the shelf, grabbed the cones across the aisle, and placed them in the basket. "Is there anything else you would like?"

"No, I think this will do nicely for now." Stella grinned as she walked beside him, enjoying being with him and doing something spontaneous like buying ice cream.

As they rounded the corner, amusement sparked in Wilder's eyes as he stopped in his tracks and motioned with his chin toward the front of the store.

Stella bit back a laugh. The Xavier-look-a-like person was ringing up customers at the checkout counter.

"Stella Nicely and Wilder Templeton!"

They both turned as Henry Doss's grandson, David Mitchell, walked toward them. They had met the young man when they had lunch at his house that day after church.

"How are you doing?" David's smiling gaze bounced back and forth between them.

"We're doing well," Wilder shook David's hand.

"Did you find everything you needed?"

Wilder nodded. "We did. Thank you."

"Great." David pointed to the man standing behind the counter. "Stella and Wilder meet my dad, Michael Mitchell."

Michael smiled. "Good to make your acquaintance. I had heard you two were living here now. I hope you're enjoying Crawdad Beach."

"We are, thank you." Amusement playing in Wilder's expression, he shook the man's hand.

Stella gave a little wave. What if they had accosted Michael at Tiddlywinks or set the authorities after him? At those thoughts, heat slid up her back. Thank goodness they had not done anything that would have made this even more awkward.

After they checked out, she walked without talking to Wilder's car. As they slid into their seats and the doors closed, Stella playfully smacked Wilder's arm. "Can you imagine if we had arrested the owner of Mitchell's grocery store?"

Wilder chuckled as he drove back to her place. "From here on out, I will let the proper authorities handle any situations in Crawdad Beach."

She grinned as she nudged him with her elbow. "I think that's very wise for both of us."

Wilder sat next to Stella on her back deck. They'd spent the last five hours talking, and he'd finally gotten her to open up and share more about her childhood. He knew she'd been raised in an orphanage but had no idea how lonely her life had been before she married Benjamin. A large birthmark on her face had kept those wanting to adopt a baby or young child from choosing Stella. She told him she had used makeup when she got old enough. The mark had faded over time, but the hurt remained. Sometimes, Wilder could see the little girl inside her still struggling to trust him or anyone else.

He understood better than Stella would ever realize.

Wilder was not proud that he'd dated so many women in the past. His heart had been ripped out and trampled by several women, and trusting didn't come easy for him either. What people didn't know is his earlier pursuit of women had stemmed from his background, which he would never discuss with anyone. The scars from his childhood were deep until God healed him. Loving Stella came with risks, but he would hope and pray for the best for both of them.

The back door opened, and Mia stepped toward them with her travel bag slung over her shoulder. "I'm heading out."

"Where are you going?" Stella asked as she stood.

Wilder stood next to the women.

"I have an assignment," Mia said. "Not sure when I'll be back. Maybe a week or two." She grinned at them both. "You two behave. I don't want to hear any rumors about you trying to arrest any more of the Crawdadians."

"We promise to be good." Stella grinned as she crossed her heart.

"Have a safe trip," Wilder said.

Mia moved close to him and whispered in his ear.

Wilder swallowed hard as she made it very clear what would happen to him if he did not treat Stella right. Mia's threats were never to be taken lightly. With all sincerity, he looked her in the eyes. "I promise."

"Good." With that, she turned and walked away.

Stella tilted her head as she surveyed him. "What did she say."

Wilder grimaced. "Not too much, other than I would lose

a body part or two if I don't treat you like a lady."

Stella sucked in a breath. "I'm sorry. I would say her bark is worse than her bite, but you know that's not true."

"Yes, I am fully aware of Mia's capabilities." Wilder took Stella's hand in his. "I love you, Stella. I promise to do my best never to hurt you." And, with God's help, he would make good on that promise.

Chapter 24

Stella wasn't sure of the exact hour, but she knew they had been officially dating for two months and five days. The many pleasant thoughts about Wilder kept her preoccupied, which meant she could barely concentrate on her work.

Wilder had given her a safe place to process and bring to light things she had locked away from her past. He now knew more about her than anyone else, including her late husband. Benjamin had been a sweet man, and it wasn't that she had consciously kept some information from him, But somehow, Wilder seemed to be able to sympathize with her and understand how she felt. However, when she asked about his childhood, he would divert the questions to another subject. She needed to work on that and see if she could get him to open up.

"Yo, roomie, want a cinnamon roll?" Mia set a bag of pastries on Sella's desk, handed her a napkin, and plopped in the chair beside her.

"Thank you. I haven't eaten breakfast yet, and this sounds and smells wonderful."

"You staying busy?" Mia took a bite of her roll.

Stella took one for herself and breathed deep the wonderful aroma of the fresh-baked pastry. "I do have a project I'm working on, but I'm having trouble concentrating."

"I am sure you are since you're off in twitterpated, dreamy-eye, la la land. So, have you told Wilder you love him?"

"Not yet." Stella took a bite of her roll. The sweetness danced on her tongue, and the sweet thoughts of Wilder danced in her head. Oh, good grief, she was very much in love with him.

"Why are you waiting? It's obvious you two are in love."

"I don't know." Stella cringed at herself. She knew it had to be hard on Wilder that she didn't respond when he said he loved her. "Saying the words is a big step."

"Well, put on your big girl panties and take that step. Poor Wilder having to wait. How long have you been dating?"

"A little over two months."

Mia's eyes narrowed as she leaned toward her. "You love Wilder, right?" When Stella nodded, Mia continued. "Then tell him. Why are you not being honest with your feelings?"

Shoving a big bite of the pastry in her mouth, Stella tried to avoid making eye contact with her friend. She wanted to tell Wilder she loved him, but the words kept sticking in her throat. Why was that? Maybe she felt guilty loving another man after Benjamin. Or, perhaps she felt like she didn't deserve to love another man. Whatever the reason, she had held back telling Wilder her true feelings.

Mia took a deep breath and leaned back in her chair. "Years ago, Wilder and I dated for a few months."

Stella's stomach dropped. "What? I didn't know that."

"Yep." Mia grinned and nodded. "We did the dating thing. Movies, dinner, etcetera."

Stella's stomach churned as heat rose up her back. She held up her hand. "I don't want to know. Why are you telling me this?"

Mia leaned toward her, her gaze intense. "Because Wilder was a complete gentleman. We didn't even kiss or hug. Nothing. No extracurricular activities at all. We were buddies hanging out together. Wilder's reputation might not be stellar, but I think much of what was said about his escapades is not true. Wilder's always been a great-looking guy, and women made up stories about him just to make themselves look better. People talk, and gossips spread gossip. I'm telling you this because I believe you can trust Wilder as a friend and with the next steps in your relationship."

"Next steps?"

"Do I have to spell it out? It's time for you two to settle down and enjoy a long-term, committed relationship. In other words, tell Wilder you love him and get married. Get a puppy or kitty and have a fur baby. Stay in Crawdad Beach, travel the world, or do both. Just stop dragging your feet and jump in."

Stella whimpered at the thought. She did love Wilder, but really loving in a forever, every day, and every night kind of way was a huge step. Part of her wanted to squeal in excitement; the other part reminded her she wasn't young anymore. Plus, her body wasn't the same as when she was younger, and she might even snore. Love comes with huge risks, but if she didn't take the risk, she might never have the pleasure of truly loving Wilder.

Mia chuckled. "Well, I can see your brain is firing away on all cylinders, trying to figure out the pros and cons of love. Give it up, girlfriend. No one has been able to decipher that issue. Love is love, and when love comes calling, especially someone like Wilder who loves you and shares your faith, pray for wisdom and open your heart to however God leads."

Stella took a shuddering breath. "Okay, I need to finish this project and then spend some time in prayer. Wilder is meeting me at Tiddlywinks at noon. I'll tell him after we eat."

Mia grinned and shimmied her shoulders. "I expect to hear a good report later today." Humming a love song, she sashayed out of the door.

Putting her head in her hands, Stella whimpered a prayer for help, guidance, wisdom, and bravery.

Tempting smells met Wilder as he stepped inside Tiddlywinks restaurant and looked to see if Stella was already there. He spotted her in the back. She stared at the menu and didn't see him as he approached.

"Hey, beautiful. Is this seat taken?"

Stella lifted her gaze to him, and her grin looked a touch mischievous. "I'm sorry, the chair is reserved for the gentleman I'm dating."

"I bet I can take him." Wilder sat across from her and

raised an eyebrow in challenge.

"I don't know. The man I'm dating is a courageous and handsome man with a very specific set of skills."

"He is, is he? I bet I can still take him." Wilder bit back his grin as he cracked his knuckles. "For your hand, fair maiden, I would challenge the man to a duel at dawn."

"For me? Why, dear sir, I can't imagine you would fight for me." Stella dramatically fanned herself.

Thoroughly enjoying the banter, Wilder leaned toward her and gazed into her gorgeous green eyes. "For the woman I love, I will fight to the death."

Stella took a deep breath, bit her lip, then rose to her feet and leaned beside his ear. "You are the man I love. I love you, Wilder Templeton."

He jumped up, wrapped her in his arms, and gave her a kiss he hoped would seal their love forever.

The sound of applause brought him back to his senses. People in the restaurant were applauding, hooting, and hollering.

An older woman at the table beside them wiped her eyes and shouted. "She said yes! Oh, this is so sweet."

Wilder swallowed hard. They thought he had asked her to marry him? Stella's eyes rounded as she stared at him. What was he going to do now?

Chapter 25

Obviously, she should have waited to say she loved him in a more private location. Stella stared at Wilder. The man's face was beet red; he looked like he would pass out and stood still as if he couldn't move. What was he thinking? For a man who had to be quick on his feet with his previous job, he seemed glued to the floor—poor guy.

She nudged him with her elbow and whispered. "There is no pressure to do anything, okay? Let's just eat our meal and quietly go about our day."

Moving wooden-like, he nodded and waited until she sat before settling across from her. A waitress came to take their order while gushing over how special it was to witness their engagement.

Wilder waited until the waitress left and leaned toward Stella. "I'm sorry I overreacted when you said you love me. I loved hearing you say that. But I'm sorry if everybody thinks we're engaged now. I mean, not that I wouldn't be thrilled if we were engaged, but this isn't how I would want to propose. I'd rather do something big like rent an airplane and have the words written in the sky, take you up in a hot air balloon, or dine in the finest restaurant by the beach. "

Stella grinned. "Wilder Templeton, have you been giving

this some thought?"

"You would be surprised how many thoughts I have about me asking you to marry me?"

"Oh, my." Heat igniting in her cheeks, Stella fanned herself for real. It might have taken her two months to say she loved Wilder, but she wouldn't mind if they moved to the next level. "I wouldn't expect a fancy engagement." Stella sucked in a breath. She didn't mean to say that out loud.

"You wouldn't?"

Stella shook her head. "No." Might as well jump in and see what happened next. She held her hand toward his. "I love you, and I love being with you."

Wilder wrapped her fingers in his. "I love you and love being with you too."

"Excuse me." A short, round woman with silver hair and plump cheeks smiled at them with the broadest, sweetest smile Stella had ever seen. "Congratulations on your engagement. I'm Faith Hollis. My husband and I own the restaurant and want to pay for your meal. We haven't had an engagement in here in at least five years."

Stella giggled as she looked at Wilder's red face and wide eyes. She turned her attention back to the woman. "Thank you for the kind offer, but..." Stella bit her lip as she tried to think of something to say.

Wilder swallowed hard, stood beside Faith, and whispered in her ear.

The woman's eyes widened, then quickly recovered. Faith patted Wilder's arm, whispered something back to him, and smiled at them both. "Don't worry about the bill, it's on us." Her shoulders raised as she gave a happy sigh. "You do make a lovely couple. Enjoy your time together." She gave them a little wave, then hurried away.

Before Stella could ask Wilder what they had whispered about, a steady stream of people stopped by their table to congratulate them. Some people even remembered Wilder from the bakery bomb incident and thanked him for saving their town.

Wilder shook hands, and Stella thanked each one as her thoughts went in a zillion directions. From the look on Wilder's face, he was doing some powerful thinking himself. They had definitely gotten themselves in a predicament. What would happen next since news in Crawdad Beach traveled fast? There was no telling who would show up on her doorstep with congratulations on their engagement.

The waitress brought their food and even had a helium congratulations balloon that she tied to Stella's chair.

They both thanked the young woman, but poor Wilder just stared at his food and didn't even pick up his fork.

Stella didn't mean to giggle, but she couldn't help it. The whole situation was amusing. Under the table, she nudged his foot with hers. "I haven't had this much fun in ages."

Wilder raised his gaze to hers. "I'm grateful because I haven't been this embarrassed in ages."

"You don't have to be embarrassed about anything. Everybody made assumptions about our situation. Which you have to admit is kind of funny."

"Maybe it will be in a few years," Wilder mumbled.

As he quietly ate, Stella wished she could peer into his brain and decipher his thoughts.

His head popped up, and he sent her a grin. "How about after lunch, I drop you off at your place and pick you up at about five? Then we can get a light supper and take a stroll on the beach. Dress casual, and we will enjoy our evening without the whole town looking over at us and smiling all dreamy-eyed."

Stella glanced around the room. "At least they are smiling."

"Good point." Wilder nodded. "But we better finish eating and get out of here before the truth comes out."

"Why are you stopping here?" Wilder stared at the well-maintained brick house in a nice neighborhood closer to the beach. "Are you sure about this? I thought we would be going to a store."

Chester parked his car in the driveway. "My friend is in the business but doesn't have a storefront."

Wilder shot him a look. "When Faith Hollis told me you were the man to see about engagement rings, I thought you would take me somewhere legit."

Turning off the car, Chester rubbed his forehead like he had a headache. "Why does everyone doubt me? My friend is an old army buddy. After his time in the service, he had a jewelry store. He's now retired, but he still likes to help out his friends and family. I'm his friend, so here we are. I called him, and he's expecting us and has some items for you to consider. Whatever you do, don't try to pet his dogs. They will chew off your hand or face."

Chapter 26

Stella chewed on her fingernails as she stared at the clothes in her closet. Forcing her hands to her side, she tried to make a decision. Wilder had told her to dress comfortably, but she didn't want to be too casual if he proposed. And even more awkward, what if he didn't?

After the scene in the restaurant, the whole town probably thought they were engaged. Would Wilder feel rushed and pushed to ask her to marry him? Part of her would cry if he didn't pop the question, and the other part would... Stella paused as the realization hit her. She *really* did want to be married to Wilder.

Why did it take her two months to tell him she loved him when she was ready to make such a big step? Maybe because, to her, love meant a committed relationship. The thought of being with Wilder in marriage was wonderful, exciting, and terrifying.

"You should wear the green sundress."

Stella jolted to find Mia standing next to her. When had she come into the room, and how long had she been there?

Her friend grinned as she took the dress out of the closet and held it against Stella. "The green one makes your eyes stand out."

"Stand out in a good way?"

"Of course." Mia gave her an incredulous look. "I wouldn't dress you funny unless I were competing with you for Wilder's affections. Then, I would have you dress in something *very* unflattering."

Insecurities attacking, Stella glanced at her friend. "You don't have feelings for him, do you?"

Mia waved her hand. "Please, don't even go there. Wilder is a great-looking guy, and he's a great person, but my only feelings for him are brotherly, and that's all they have ever been. And don't worry. Wilder saw me only as a friend and sister-type, too, and nothing romantic. He's all yours. Now, get yourself ready and enjoy your evening."

Twenty minutes later, Stella was dressed and ready to go as she peered out her front window. This could be one of the biggest days of her life or just a regular date. Either way, she needed to calm down. She took a deep breath, blew it out, and did it again and again until she was getting lightheaded. Feeling way too woozy, Stella sat on the couch.

What if Wilder didn't ask her to marry him? She wasn't even sure how to pray other than God's will to be done, and she sure hoped His will was in line with what she hoped would happen.

Dinner was fantastic, and walking next to Stella on the

beach as the sun set in the distance couldn't have made for a more perfect evening. A light breeze kept it from being too hot, and most people had left for the day so they could walk in peace. However, Stella seemed distant, as though something was on her mind. She even looked disappointed when they left the restaurant.

Stella squeezed his hand. "I heard you dated Mia."

Wilder laughed. "Dating Mia? You're kidding, right?" Maybe that's what was worrying Stella.

She glanced at him, and he could see the hurt or insecurity in her gaze. "No, she said you dated for a few months but that you had been a perfect gentleman."

Wilder gave her a reassuring look. "We went out together, but I wouldn't call it dating. Mia is attractive and nice, but she's scary. That woman could take on an army and win." He shuddered. "She's a friend, more like a buddy, not dating material. Nope." He stopped and pulled Stella into a hug. "You don't have anything to worry about. You are the one I'm dating and the woman I love. "

Stella leaned against him. "I love you too." Her voice was only a whisper.

How he wished she would understand how much he loved her. He rubbed his hand along her back, loving the feel of her next to him. In the distance, music played at a restaurant farther down the beach. He swayed to the melody, and their embrace turned into a slow dance.

Stella sighed against him, moving in time like they had danced together for years.

Wilder's cell rang, and he apologized as he begrudgingly stepped away. He disconnected the call and took Stella's hand. "I'm really sorry, but I need to get back to town and take care of something."

Stella nodded as moisture built in her eyes.

Oh, man, he was screwing everything up. He took her back in his arms and kissed her. "I love you, Stella. Please don't be upset. It's going to be okay."

Stella sniffled and stiffened. "I'm fine. It's okay, I understand." She wiggled out of his arms and walked toward where he had parked.

Wilder internally groaned as he caught up with her. She didn't look at him as she hurried to his car and let herself inside.

Praying he hadn't messed up a wonderful evening, he drove back to Crawdad Beach. He tried to keep a conversation going, but Stella's responses were only yes or no.

At her house, he sent up a silent prayer for help as he walked her to the door. "I'm sorry again for cutting short our time together. Can I come inside for a few minutes?"

All Stella wanted to do was go to her room and cry. The meal was great, spending time with him was great, and dancing with him on the beach was wonderful, but she thought Wilder would have asked her to marry him. She tried to keep her lip from trembling. She shouldn't be so upset, but she was. Trying to get out of her rotten mood, Stella nodded in response to Wilder's question about coming inside for a few minutes.

She opened the door and stopped. Why was it so dark? Where was Mia? She should still be here. Stella sighed and flipped on the lights, and gasped.

Soft music played one of her favorite songs from when she was younger, and a massive bouquet of roses sat on the coffee table. Across the room hung a big sign that read, *Will you marry me?*

Fighting tears, Stella turned to Wilder.

Kneeling, he held out a velvet box containing a gorgeous round-cut diamond ringed in emeralds. "Stella Nicely, and whatever name may be on your birth certificate, will you marry me?"

Crying, laughing, and rejoicing, she held her hand toward him. "Yes!"

Wilder put the ring on her finger, gently wrapped his arms around her, and swayed to the music.

Epilogue

Six months.

For six glorious months, she had been the wife of Wilder Templeton. Stella gave a happy sigh as she sat on the couch and rubbed Butch's soft fur. Wilder had named their little Bichon puppy, hoping he would grow up to be a brut. Contrary to the little dog's name, he was a lover, not a fighter. What tickled her was that Wilder was even more affectionate with the pup than she was. She couldn't believe how much she enjoyed being a dog mom.

After their private sunset wedding on the beach, Wilder took her on a honeymoon to the Caribbean, and then they moved into another house in Crawdad Beach. Surprisingly, Mia had bought Stella's other home and was in and out as she continued to go on missions doing whatever she did.

Wilder carried two mugs of coffee and handed Stella one. "What time are we meeting the family?" He settled next to her.

Stella wanted to giggle at the thought. "Six o'clock at David and Marie's house. I still need to make a casserole to take with us. I can't believe all the wonderful things that have happened these last few months."

Wilder's smile mischievous, he raised an eyebrow. "Besides the thrill of marrying me, what could be better?"

Stella laughed as she nudged him with her elbow. "You are one of the best and favorite things to happen to me."

He leaned toward her and kissed her. "Mrs. Templeton, you are my very best and most favorite forever."

After the fantastic kiss, Stella sipped her coffee. Surely, she was the happiest woman on earth. Besides having Wilder as her husband, last month, Henry Doss's family convinced Henry and Stella to send in their DNA to see if they were related. They were convinced her green eyes had to be a connection since Henry's mom had the same eye color. Stella thought it was a ridiculous idea, but she was shocked to discover that Henry was indeed her older half-brother.

God had been so incredibly gracious to her. Jude and Loraine had been given life sentences, so Stella no longer needed to worry about that problem. And now, she not only had a wonderful husband, she had been blessed with a wonderful family.

With a happy sigh, Stella grinned toward the ceiling and internally prayed her thanks to her good and loving Heavenly Father.

The End

To the Reader

Thank you for taking the time to read *Stella's Heart Code.* Writing stories for me is always an adventure. I have some ideas about my main characters and know there will always be a happy ending, yet I am clueless about how the story will unfold. Maybe you were as surprised as I was as some scenes played out.

I hope you have enjoyed the Crawdad Beach series. I just wish the little town wasn't fictional, and we could sit and visit with the characters.

Perhaps, like Stella in the book's first part, you are alone. Would you like to join the absolute best forever family? I have good news. Life is hard and often heartbreaking, but God is good, and with Christ in your life, you will always get a happy ending. For God loved the world so much that He gave His only Son (Jesus Christ) so that everyone who believes in Him will not perish but have eternal life. And as many who receive and believe in Jesus Christ, God gives them the right to become children of God. Oh, how great a love the Father has given us, that we can be called children of God (John 3:16, 1:12, 1 John 3:1).

If you liked the book, would you be so kind as to leave a positive review or tell your friends? As an author, hearing someone likes my stories makes the long hours of living in a fictional world worth every minute. And, for every positive review given, the Crawdadians of Crawdad Beach will send their thanks.

Acknowledgments

To my loving Heavenly Father, thank You for grace and mercy. Thank you for the stories You have blessed me to write.

My sweet husband, Dennis, thank you for loving me even when I spent hours and hours hanging out with my imaginary Crawdad Beach friends.

Patricia (PacJac) Carroll, thank you for your friendship, edits, suggestions, and the fun ways you motivate me to continue writing.

Jack Foster, thank you again for the creative Crawdad drawings you blessed me with to use throughout the Crawdad Beach Series. Readers, please visit Jack at jackfosterart.com

Readers, thank you for taking the time to read my books!

About the Author

Lisa Buffaloe is a happily married mom, multi-published author, and speaker. Lisa enjoys spending time with God, writing, hanging out with her sweet husband, and enjoying God's beautiful nature.

Visit Lisa at https://lisabuffaloe.com

Books by Lisa
Fiction
Stella's Heart Code
A Baker's Heart
Crystal's Journey Home
Visible, yet Hidden
Running to Grace
The Masterpiece Beneath
Nadia's Hope
Prodigal Nights
Writing Her Heart
The Discovery Chapter
Open Lens
The Fortune
Grace for the Char-Baked

Non-Fiction
Float by Faith
Heart and Soul Medication
Time with The Timeless One

The Forgotten Resting Place
Present in His Presence
We Were Meant for Paradise
One Lit Step: Devotions for your journey
The Unnamed Devotional
Flying on His Wings
Unfailing Treasures
No Wound Too Deep For The Deep Love of Christ
Living Joyfully Free Devotional (Volumes 1 & 2)

Thank you for reading,

Stella's Heart Code

Lisa Buffaloe

www.ingramcontent.com/pod-product-compliance
Lightning Source LLC
Chambersburg PA
CBHW072229190626
46809CB00017B/1531

* 9 7 8 1 9 5 7 7 1 5 2 7 8 *